America's Controversies:

The Death Penalty, Clinton's Presidency and Export of Democracy to Nicaragua

By
Ksenija Arsic

Llumina Press

© 2005 Ksenija Arsic

All rights reserved. No part of this publication may be reproduced or transmitted in any form or by any means electronic or mechanical, including photocopy, recording, or any information storage and retrieval system, without permission in writing from both the copyright owner and the publisher.

Requests for permission to make copies of any part of this work should be mailed to Permissions Department, Llumina Press, PO Box 772246, Coral Springs, FL 33077-2246

ISBN: 1-59526-480-9 PB
       1-59526-481-7 HC

Printed in the United States of America by Llumina Press

Library of Congress Control Number: 2005935590

Dedication

To my wonderful husband, Zoran Arsic, and our precious daughter, Viktorija Arsic – thank you for all your love and support.

To my mother, Gordana Miskovic and my father, Milenko Mihajlovic, – thank you for everything that you have taught me.

To my dear friend Ljiljana Trisovic-Felbab – thank you for always being there for me.

Table of Contents

Killing the Killers in an Advanced Society:
Why America Still Supports the Death Penalty

Introduction — i

Chapter One

The Importance and Use of DNA Testing in Capital Cases — 1

Capital Punishment, post conviction DNA testing, and the flaws of the American criminal justice system

Chapter Two

The American vs. the International Stance on Capital Punishment — 21

The distinction between the views held by American/Canadian society and Western European nations regarding the death penalty

Chapter Three

The Procedural Obstacles in the Path of the Last Hope — 37

The restrictions upheld by the Supreme Court and Congress on federal Habeas Corpus in capital cases

Conclusion — 45

Appendix A — 49

Appendix B — 51

Appendix C — 53

Bibliography — 55

Articles and Publications — 65

Web Pages	67
Assessing the Legacy of Bill Clinton's Presidency	71

Will he be remembered for more than just the issues surrounding his impeachment?

Introduction	71
Evaluating the Presidents of the United States of America	75
The Clinton Presidency before the Impeachment	85
Clinton's Legacy after Leaving Office	93
Conclusion	95
Bibliography	99
The American Dream	105
American Foreign Policy towards Cuba	109
The Future of the U.S. – Cuba Relations and the Lesson to Be Learned	111
The Transition to Democracy in Nicaragua	113
Introduction	113
Definitions of Democracy, Transition, and Consolidation	117
Nicaragua	123
Conclusion	131
Bibliography	133

Killing the Killers in an Advanced Society:
Why America Still Supports the Death Penalty

Introduction

A profoundly controversial and complicated issue concerning the application of the death penalty in the United States seems destined to remain unresolved for generations to come. Every election year, American politicians – wishing to appeal to the moral sentiments of voters – routinely compete with each other as to who will be toughest in extending the death penalty to those persons who have been convicted of the most heinous crimes.[1]

In an attempt to answer a variety of philosophical, moral, ethical and legal questions surrounding this ultimate and irreversible punishment, both proponents and opponents of capital punishment present compelling arguments to support their claims. The dispute over the death penalty in America remains a significant one – and, apparently, it is far from reaching any reasonable resolution acceptable to both sides.[2] According to Stewart Banner, there are two possible solutions: either the Supreme Court simplifies the states' procedures for sentencing criminals to death or state legislators take a stand and abolish capital punishment.[3]

---

[1] See "Beyond Repair? Americas Death Penalty," edited by Stephen P. Garvey, Chapter 1: "Second Thoughts: Americans' Views on the Death Penalty at the turn of the century," (Durham and London, Duke University Press, 2003), Pg. 44. " Crime became a major item on the national political agenda in 1968, when Richard Nixon made 'law and order' a prime focus of his campaign for President. Nixon was not the first to make crime an issue in a Presidential campaign. Republican candidate Barry Goldwater did so in his unsuccessful campaign in 1964, and the concept of a 'War against the crime' originated in the second Johnson administration, 1965-1969."

[2] See Kenneth C. Haas and James A. Inciardi,"Challenging Capital Punishment, Legal and Social Science Approaches," (Newbury Park, Beverly Hills, London, New Delhi: Sage Publications, 1988), Pg.7-11.

[3] See Stuart Banner, "The Death penalty: An American History," (Cambridge: Harvard University Press, 2002), Pg.310.

Throughout the centuries, capital punishment has evolved in both form and function. Through the 17th and 18th centuries, the death penalty was standard for a variety of crimes such as arson, horse theft, forgery, burglary and even adultery. The common method of execution was hanging.[4] Capital punishment enjoyed an overarching space in most societies throughout the globe not only because it was believed to be a righteous sentencing but because hangings served as an intriguing public spectacle for people of all ages, races and social classes. The purpose of public execution was, first, to serve as a deterrent for other potential criminals, second, as a measure of retribution and, third, as the opportunity for the condemned person to express his or her remorse. These events were carefully controlled and carried out by authorities.[5]

In the late 18th century, the concept of the prison was born – marking a change in attitude regarding the death penalty in America. Public executions were no longer preformed on the streets. Instead, they were administered in a jail yard with few witnesses. A movement opposing the number and frequency of death sentences also began to arise during this period. A growing number of people believed that the death penalty was being applied too often and for too many crimes. By the middle of the 19th century, three states – Michigan, Rhode Island and Wisconsin – managed to abolish the death penalty for murder. These were the first states to do so before the Civil War.[6]

---

[4] See Hugo Adam Bedau, 3rd ed. "The Death Penalty in America," Chapter 1: "Background and Developments," (New York: Oxford University Press, 1982), Pg. 3-28.

[5] See Louis P. Masur, "Rites of Execution, Capital Punishment and the transformation of American culture, 1776-1865," (New York, Oxford: Oxford University Press, 1989). Also see Stuart Banner, "The Death penalty: An American History," (Cambridge: Harvard University Press, 2002), Pg. 62-70.

[6] See Hugo Adam Bedau, 3d ed. "The Death Penalty in America," Chapter 1: "Background and Developments, See Hugo Adam Bedau, 3rd ed. "The Death Penalty in America," Chapter 1: "Background and Developments," (New York: Oxfor University Press, 1982), Pg. 3-28..

[6] See Louis P. Masur, "Rites of Execution, Capital Punishment and the transformation of American culture, 1776-1865," (New York, Oxford: Oxford University Press, 1989). Also see Stuart Banner, "The Death penalty: An American History," (Cambridge: Harvard University Press, 2002), Pg. 62-70.

[6] See Hugo Adam Bedau, 3d ed. "The Death Penalty in America," Chapter 1: "Background and Developments," (New York: Oxford University Press, 1982), Pg. 21-24.

This same progression was paralleled by the sharp upward curve in technological advancement. With each new technological discovery came a new way to carry out executions. The introduction of electricity in the late 18th century resulted in the electric chair, followed by the gas chamber. This period also stewarded in the introduction of trained professionals, hired to oversee each execution. In the long run, these changes – despite being masked as representative of a steady search for more humane alternatives to hanging – were little more than new and improved methods to perpetuate the centralization of capital punishment.

Today, this array of methods has been applied to an entirely new use. Several U.S. states now offer their death row inmates the chance to choose their own method of execution. A prisoner has the opportunity to choose between electrocution, asphyxiation, and the modern technique of lethal injection. [7]

The first constitutional challenge to capital punishment – championed by the American Civil Liberties Union and the Legal Defense Fund – reached the Supreme Court in 1972. In, *Furman v. Georgia,* five Justices ruled that the capital sentencing statutes of every state violated the cruel and unusual punishment clause of the 8th and 14th Amendments; hence, the practice was unconstitutional.[8] This decision was short-lived, however. By the end of the 20th century, the ruling had been overturned.

Americans pride themselves on their commitment to human rights. Ironically, in vigorously applying the death penalty, the U.S finds itself in company with several countries that are counted among the worst human rights abusers in the world. In recent years, the top five employers of capital punishment were China, the Democratic Republic of Congo, Iran, Saudi Arabia and the United States. American supporters of the practice defend this most ignoble distinction by comparing the deadly methods employed by the top five offenders. In the US, convicted criminals are put to a death by lethal injection –

---

[7] See William A. Schabas, "The Death Penalty As Cruel Treatment and Torture, Capital Punishment Challenged in the World's Courts," "Method of Execution" (Boston: Northeastern University Press, 1996), Pg. 157-201. Also see Appendix B of this book.

[8] See Stuart Banner, "The Death penalty: An American History," (Cambridge: Harvard University Press, 2002), Pg. 266. Also see Hugo Adam Bedau, 3d ed. "The Death Penalty in America," (New York: Oxford University Press, 1982) Pg.253-304.

which is commonly perceived as the highest (or most "humane") way of execution. [9] Contrary evidence was reported by the British medical journal, *The Lancet*. According to the study, three U.S. anesthesiologists and one lawyer concluded that, "lethal injection anesthesia methodology is flawed and some inmates might have experienced awareness and suffering during execution."[10]

In addition, there are increased and equally disturbing findings of innocence among the condemned – because of the introduction of DNA testing. According to the Innocence Project – created by Barry C. Scheck and Peter J. Neufeld in 1992 – DNA testing is largely responsible for the reversal of many capital convictions as well as the major shift in criminal justice legislation over the past decade. At the time of the initial findings, only New York and Illinois had legislation dealing specifically with post conviction DNA testing. [11]

The issue of wrongful convictions, which are not isolated (and certainly are not rare events), has played and will continue to play a big role in the American political arena. Perhaps the best illustration for this argument (and clearly a historical one) is the blanket commutation of all 167 death row inmates issued by Illinois Governor George Ryan on January 12, 2003.[12] Prior to this decision, a conservative Republican and a supporter of capital punishment, Governor Ryan was so troubled by the numbers (12 of 61 men found innocent of their crimes had been released from death row) that he declared moratorium on further executions.

Interestingly enough, the discovery of the erroneous convictions was not the fruit of a legal effort but, rather, the work of journalism

---

[9] See Amnesty International, "When the State Kills, The death penalty: a human rights issue," The death penalty worldwide, the USA," (New York: Amnesty International USA, 1989) Pg. 95-239. Also see Amnesty International, Death Penalty Around the World: Facts and Figures on the Death Penalty (April 2000, 2001, and 2003), http://www.amnesty-usa.org/abolish/world.html, Visited on April 7, 2003. Also see Appendix B of this book.

[10] See the National Coalition to Abolish the Death Penalty, http://hq.demaction.org/dia/organizations/ncadp/content.jsp?content_KEY=459 Visited on May 26, 2005.

[11] See Barry Scheck Peter Neufeld and Jim Dwyer," Actual Innocence, When Justice Goes wrong and how to make it right," (New York: A Signet Book, New American Library, 2000).

[12] Governor Ryan's speech on the blanket commutation of Illinois Death Row inmates, hhttp://www.stopcapitalpunishment.org/ryans_speach.html, visited on Jan. 12/2003. Also see: Illinois coalition against the death penalty, http://www.icadp.org/Pg.74.html, visited on Jan.12/2003.

students from Northwestern University. Furthermore – as Governor Ryan noted in his speech on the blanket commutation of Illinois death row inmates – a report by The Chicago Tribune clearly documented the systemic failures of the capital punishment system in Illinois:[13] *"Half of the nearly 300 capital cases in Illinois had been reversed for a new trial or re-sentencing. Nearly half!"*[14] said Governor Ryan in his speech on the blanket commutation of Illinois death row inmates. The Governor also highlighted the core reasons behind his historic decision. They are as follows:

> *I started with this issue concerned about innocence. But, once I studied, once I pondered what had become of our justice system, I came to care above all about fairness. Fairness is fundamental to the American system of justice and our way of life...If the system was making so many errors in determining whether someone was guilty in the first place, how fairly and accurately was it determining which guilty defendants deserved to live and which deserved to die? What effect was race having? What effect was poverty having? Supreme Court Justice Potter Stewart has said that the imposition of the death penalty on defendants in this country is as freakish and arbitrary as who gets hit by a bolt of lightning.*[15]

Inadequate representation is also common in other states. As stated in the Innocence Project, defendants in capital cases are often unable to pay for expert counsel. They must rely on public defenders or inexperienced and poorly paid court-appointed lawyers.[16]

Perhaps the possibility of innocent people being put to death for crimes they did not commit is itself sufficient evidence for the abolition of capital punishment. In reality, however, many supporters of the death

---

[13] Illinois coalition against the death penalty, http://www.icadp.org/Pg.74.html, Visited on Jan.12/2003.
[14] Governor Ryan's speech on the blanket commutation of Illinois Death Row inmates, hhttp://www.stopcapitalpunishment.org/ryans_speach.html, visited on Jan. 12/2003
[15] Ibid.
[16] See Barry Scheck Peter Neufeld and Jim Dwyer,"Actual Innocence, When Justice Goes wrong and how to make it right," (New York: A Signet Book, New American Library, 2000). Also see: About this Innocence Project, http://www.innocenceproject.org/about/index.php Visited on Jan.10/2003.

penalty are still unimpressed by the aforementioned argument. For example, Senator Jeremiah Denton of Alabama stated:

> *...but saying that we should not have the death penalty because we may accidentally execute an innocent man is like saying that we should not have automobiles because some innocent people might be accidentally killed in them. Or we should not have trucking or we should not have aircraft or we should not have elevators because we are going to have accidents. There are to be some mistakes committed. The question is, on balance, which way do we better promote the general welfare?* [17]

Nevertheless, what evidence does Senator Denton offer that the death penalty does indeed contribute to the betterment of society? Supporters of capital punishment have called for new laws to blanket the penalty and cut down on error. Unfortunately, countless of the "new" penalty laws cannot fix the obvious flaws in the American justice system. [18]

The purpose of this study is twofold. First, it will posit that the history of the death penalty has never suggested any benefit to a civilized society – and that it is, in fact, conducive to a heightened tolerance for violence among the general population. Second, it will reflect upon the number of innocent people sentenced to death in America by a legal system that clearly is not without flaw – and, as with any just-cause argument, will attempt to display that, without an infallible legal system, there cannot justly exist an irreversible sentencing practice. In other words, for retention of capital punishment, or for it to be legitimate and accepted at all, the American system of justice has to ensure an absolute certainty and consistency of the death penalty application and that seems to be unachievable..

The first Chapter of this paper will address the importance of the use of DNA testing in capital cases and how this evolving practice affects the topics of inadequate legal representation, racial prejudice, and other flaws in the American criminal justice system. In Chapter Two, this study will examine the stark discrepancy in the practice of

---

[17] See Stuart Banner, "The Death penalty: An American History," (Cambridge: Harvard University Press, 2002), Pg.304.

[18] See Amnesty International, "When the State Kills, The death penalty: a human rights issue," Cover Pg., (New York: Amnesty International USA, 1989). See also, Hugo Adam Bedau 3d Ed. "The Death Penalty in America," (New York: Oxford University Press, 1982), Pg.37- 47.

capital punishment between the United States and the rest of the Western industrialized countries. The repercussions to the U.S. in the event of a global decision to abolish capital punishment – an event that, conceivably, could be just over the horizon – will also be discussed.

In Chapter Three, this study will examine *Habeas Corpus*. While this is a time-tested method to weeding out many errors of the American legal system, it is perhaps time to consider significant revision.

Revision – at least where the death penalty is concerned – has been steadily working its way into the American arena. Recently, the Supreme Court ruled that it is unconstitutional to execute developmentally disabled people. The Court has also ruled that a jury, not a judge, should decide on the presence or absence of factors that make a case eligible for the death penalty. Furthermore, two federal judges in unrelated cases held that the existing death penalty is unconstitutional. The most recent decision of the U.S. Supreme Court, on March 1, 2005 in *Roper v. Simmons*, invalidates the death penalty for juvenile offenders:

> *In a 5-4 opinion delivered by Justice Anthony Kennedy, the Court ruled that standards of decency have evolved so that executing minors is "cruel and unusual punishment" prohibited by the Eighth Amendment. The majority cited a consensus against the juvenile death penalty among state legislatures, and its own determination that the death penalty is a disproportionate punishment for minors. Finally, the Court pointed to "overwhelming" international opinion against the juvenile death penalty.* [19]

Can these rulings be interpreted as a signal of a fundamental shift in the court's stance on the death penalty – as well as the possibility for a change in American public opinion and even governmental policy? By Sarat's account, there is a fundamental assumption that the answer to these questions might be affirmative; "The new abolitionism to stop one line of killing, namely capital punishment, asks us to do so in the hope that our present embrace of the killing state is the result of fear rather than venality, misunderstanding rather than clear-headed commitment." [20]

---

[19] See: OYEZ, U.S. Supreme Court Multimedia, Roper v. Simmons, 543 U.S. ___ (2005) Docket Number: 03-633, Abstract
http://www.oyez.org/oyez/resource/case/1724/, Visited on March 2, 2005.

[20] See Sarat Austin: "When the state kills, Capital punishment and the American Condition," Chapter 9: "Conclusion: Toward a new abolitionism," (Princeton, New Jersey: Princeton University Press, 2001), pg.260.

Chapter One

The Importance and Use of DNA Testing in Capital Cases

Capital punishment, post conviction DNA testing and the flaws of the American criminal justice system

The increased use of forensic DNA testing in capital cases has led to the exoneration of more than a hundred death row inmates in recent years, causing U.S. citizens to take a serious second look at the reliability and fairness of the American criminal justice system.[21] According to the Gallup Poll Organization,

---

[21] See Governor George H. Rayan's speech (Jan.11, 2003) on the blanket commutation of Illinois Death Row inmates.
http://www.stopcapitalpunishment.org/ryans_speach.html, visited on Jan.12/2003. "Since we reinstated the death penalty there are also 93 people, 93, where our criminal justice system imposed the most severe sanction and later rescinded the sentence or even released them from custody because they were innocent. How many more cases of wrongful conviction have to occur before we can all agree that the system is broken?" Also see Barry Scheck, Peter Neufeld and Jim Dwyer, Actual Innocence, When Justice Goes wrong and how to make it right. (New York: A Signet Book, New American Library, 2000), Introduction, Pg. xxii. "Some six thousand people have been sent to death row since 1976. as of this writing, eighty-eight of them have been cleared trough variety of means, including DNA tests. " Some people think that an error rate of one percent is acceptable for the death penalty," notes Kevin Doyle, the capital defender for the state of New York." But if you went to the FAA and ask them to approve an airplane, and you said, oh, by the way on every one hundredth landing, it causes or almost causes fatalities, people would say you were nuts." See also Causes and

1

however, the majority of Americans still strongly support capital punishment – even when it has been revealed to them that innocent people have been executed.

> *Beginning in the 1980s, the number of prisoners on death row began to rise, and has nearly tripled since then (from 691 in 1980 to 3,711 in 2001). At the same time, Americans' support for the death penalty continued to increase over the next couple decades, pushing past 70% in 1985 and reaching a high of 80% support in 1994. Since then, support has declined, dropping to 68% in October 2001, amid reports that several death row inmates were in fact innocent of the crimes for which they were charged.[22]*

---

remedies of wrongful convictions, www.innocenceproject.org/causes/dna.php, Jan.24/2003." The American criminal justice system fails sometimes. This is not a disputed fact. One price of these failures is the loss of life and livelihood for those unfortunate enough to be wrongfully convicted. The cases of those exonerated by DNA testing have revealed disturbing trends in our criminal justice system. Some claim that the eventual exoneration of these men proves that the system works. If that were true, then justice is not being administered by our police, prosecutors, defense lawyers, or our courts. It is being dispensed by law students, journalism students, and a few concerned lawyers, organizations, and citizens. That is unacceptable."

[22] See The Gallup Organization, In-depth Analyses, The Death Penalty, support for the Death Penalty Over Time, August 2002, by Jeffrey M Jones, http://www.gallup.com, visited on Feb. 7, 2003.

Figure 1. Support for the death penalty over time

Are you in favor of the death penalty for a person convicted of murder?

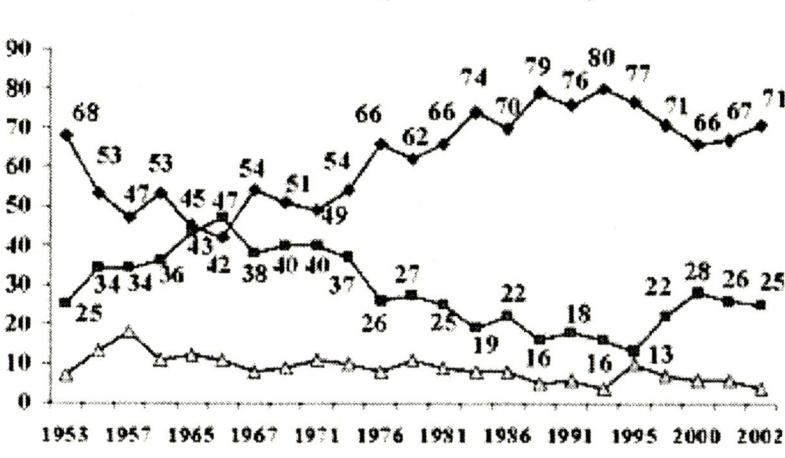

Source: The Gallup Organization, In-depth Analyses,
The Death Penalty, August 2002, by Jeffrey M. Jones.[23]

The Newsweek Poll, on the other hand, shows that 95% of Americans say that states should permit DNA testing for all death row cases, emphasizing that the states should make it easier for death row inmates to introduce new evidence that might prove their innocence. These poll results – coupled with the disturbingly frequent releases of wrongfully imprisoned inmates – could be a sign that the American public has begun to recognize the need for urgent reform of the criminal justice system.[24]

Dr. Alec Jeffreys first employed the DNA technique in Britain for a variety of social processes including immigration investigations. During the late 1980s and early 1990s, DNA technology enjoyed the

---

[23] See The Gallup Organization, In-depth Analyses, The Death Penalty, support for the Death Penalty Over Time, August 2002, by Jeffrey M Jones, http://www.gallup.com, visited on Feb. 7, 2003.

[24] See http://www.msnbc.com/news/870343.asp?0cv=KB10, Archive June 3, 2000, visited on Jan.30, 2003. Also, see Jay Robert Lifton and Greg Mitchell: "Who owns the death? Capital Punishment, the American conscience, and the end of executions," Chapter ten: "The end of executions," Pg.246. (New York, Perennial, an Imprint of Harper Collins Publishers, 2002.) "When you consider the foul-ups and mix-ups and incompetence that you often find in government work it gets scary. You realize that the institution that puts people to death is the same one that delivers the mail to the wrong people."

same impact as had fingerprinting nearly a century earlier. DNA testing has gained acceptance in the field of forensic and life sciences – as well as in the U.S. courtroom. Since 1995, the Innocence Project at the Cardozo School of Law in New York City has set up programs at 18 law schools around the country that use student volunteers to investigate cases and by applying DNA testing to win freedom for innocent persons. [25]

DNA (or deoxyribonucleic acid) is the genetic blueprint unique to a particular individual – with the exception of identical twins and bone marrow transplant recipients. If performed correctly, DNA testing can prove to be a powerful and impartial tool – able to accurately identify the perpetrator of any crimes wherein there is sufficient biological evidence. As is the case with any kind of evidence, however, there is always the potential for error – or rather, DNA cataloguing affords plenty of opportunities for mistakes (or even sabotage).[26] In 1998, Attorney General Jenet Reno established the National Commission on the Future of DNA Evidence, which created five categories for

---

[25] See Paul R. Billings M.D., Ph.D. Vice Chairman, Department of Medicine Chief, Division of Genetic Medicine, California Pacific Medical Center: " DNA on Trial, Genetic Identification and Criminal Justice," "Gene Technology: Views of its Criminal justice applications," (New York Library of Congress Cataloging-in-Publication Data, Cold Spring Harbor Laboratory Press, 1992). Pg. 1-18. Also see Barry Scheck, Peter Neufeld and Jim Dwyer," Actual Innocence, When Justice Goes wrong And how to make it right," Chapter14: "Reckonings: An Update" Pg.329-349. (New York: A Signet Book, New American Library, 2000).

[26] See Committee on DNA Technology in Forensic Science, Board on Biology, Commission on Life Sciences, National Research Council: "DNA Technology in Forensic Science" (Washington, D.C. National Academy Press, 1992), Summary, Pg. 1- 27. Also see Chapter 6: "Use of DNA Information in the Legal System"(Washington, D.C. National Academy Press, 1992). Pg.131. "To produce biological evidence that is admissible in court in criminal cases, forensic investigators must be well trained in the collection and handling of biological samples for DNA analysis. They should take care to minimize the risk of contamination and ensure that possible sources of DNA are well preserved and properly identified. As in any forensic work, they must attend to the essentials of preserving specimens, labeling, and the chain of custody and to any constitutional or statutory requirements that regulate the collection and handling of samples. The Fourth Amendment provides much of the legal framework for the gathering of DNA samples from suspects or private places, and court orders are sometimes needed in this connection." See also: " Innocence Project": "Causes and remedies of wrongful convictions," http://www.innocenceproject.org/causes/dna.php, visited on Jan.24, 2003. "Post conviction DNA Testing: Recommendations for Handling Requests," written by judges, prosecutors, defense lawyers, and victims' advocates, these guidelines provide a model that will help to ensure that only the guilty are prosecuted and convicted".

separating the types of post conviction requests.[27] For each category, the commission describes the characteristics that define those cases, provides examples, and outlines a strategy for responding to requests as follows:

Category 1 involves cases in which biological evidence was collected and still exists. If the evidence is subjected to DNA testing, favorable results will exonerate the petitioner.

Category 2 covers cases in which – even with biological evidence still available – the prosecutor might disagree as to whether the results exonerate the petitioner. This category also includes cases where, because of policy or economic reasons, there might be disagreement as to whether DNA testing should be permitted at all or, for indigent inmates, at the State's expense. The decision for testing or retesting may have to be made by a judicial officer.

Category 3 involves cases wherein evidence is subjected to DNA testing or retesting and favorable results are found to be inconclusive.

Category 4 is about cases in which biological evidence was never collected, or cannot be found, or was destroyed, or was preserved in a way that cannot be tested. In such cases, post conviction relief based on DNA testing is not possible.

Category 5 involves cases where the request for DNA testing is frivolous.[28]

The danger of DNA contamination – which renders the evidence useless – is particularly great when the investigator or researcher employs an ingenious technique known as Polymerase Chain Reaction (PCR). PCR (invented by Kary Mullis) works to create millions of exact copies of DNA from a biological sample of (for example) a single hair, body fluid, skin, particles of blood, or even from degraded DNA. Reports suggest that it is relatively simple to perform the PCR technique and results are usually obtainable within 24 hours. However, given the exceedingly sensitive nature of the PCR process, it is extremely important to ensure highly professional handling in the field and laboratory – in order to prevent a

---

[27] See Research Report:" Convicted by Juries, Exonerated by Science: Case Studies in the Use of DNA Evidence to Establish Innocent After Trial", http://www.ncjrs.org/pdffiles/dnaevid.pdf, visited on August 4, 2005. Also see: A Report from National Commission on the Future of DNA Evidence:
"Post conviction DNA Testing: Recommendations for Handling Requests", http://www.ojp.usdoj.gov/nij/, visited on August 4, 2005.

[28] Ibid.

carryover contamination that produces false or confusing results.[29] Not only is DNA evidence capable of closing a conviction for the State (even when no other evidence is available) it possesses the power to exonerate the wrongfully accused, as well. Take, for example, the cases of Earl Washington of Virginia and Frank Lee Smith of Florida.[30] Both were set free after DNA evidence authoritatively cleared their names

In many cases and for many inmates, however, it is not nearly as simple as reexamining a few blood samples. In many jurisdictions, officials have refused to authorize requests to examine DNA evidence out of fear that wrongful convictions would highlight the many wrongdoings of the criminal justice system and provide more fuel for the increasing fire to end executions.[31] Furthermore, even if access to sealed DNA evidence is granted, the defendant bears the burden to prove by preponderance of the evidence that DNA testing was not

---

[29] Ibid. "The most serious problem is contamination of evidence samples and reaction solutions with PCR products from prior amplifications. Such products can contain a target sequence at a concentration a million times greater, and even relatively small quantity should swamp the correct signal from the evidence sample. Even the simple act of flipping the top of a plastic tube might aerosolize enough DNA to pose a problem." Pg.66.

[30] See Barry Scheck, Peter Neufeld and Jim Dwyer," Actual Innocence, When Justice Goes wrong and how to make it right," Chapter 11:"The Death of Innocents" Pg.285. (New York: A Signet Book, New American Library, 2000). "In September 2000, DNA test showed that Earl Washington-a penniless mentally retarded sharecropper-was not the man who raped and killed Rebecca Lynn Williams in Culpeper, Virginia, some eighteen years earlier (fourteen of them on death row). After a drunken family brawl, police arrested Washington, who proceeded to "confess" to five crimes in the vicinity. The authorities never charged him with four of the cases, since witnesses and victims said he wasn't the assailant. Washington's confession to the murder of Mrs. Williams, a nineteen-year-old mother, was wrong about her race, the number of times she was stabbed, and the means of entry into the home. Nevertheless, he was tried and sentenced to die."See also **ACLU** on line archive: http://www.aclu.org, visited on Feb. 2, 2003. "Frank Lee Smith, Florida; Convicted 1985; cleared (after death) in 2000. Mr. Smith was convicted of the rape and murder of a child. After the trial and sentencing the chief witness recanted her testimony. But Smith nevertheless was scheduled for execution. He died of cancer in January 2000, while on death row before the completion of the DNA test results that proved his innocence ten months later."

[31] See **ACLU** on line archive: http://www.aclu.org, visited on Feb. 2, 2003. and Scheck Barry, Peter Neufeld and Jim Dwyer," Actual Innocence, When Justice Goes wrong and how to make it right," Chapter 11:"The Death of Innocents" Pg.282 (New York: A Signet Book, New American Library, 2000). "Despite this chillingly high rate of error, courts at every level are being pressured to shut their doors to death row appeals, just as more and more windows are opening to reveal capital mistakes."

originally performed because it was unavailable or technologically inadequate, and that if the DNA testing had been performed, the defendant would not have been prosecuted or convicted. Right now only two states – Illinois and New York – have laws allowing prisoners the right to post-conviction DNA analysis. Neufeld and Scheck propose that either the federal government or every state should adopt legislation to permit post-conviction DNA testing – a process that should be paid in full by the government.[32]

In 1998, the FBI created the National DNA Index System – a system that links the DNA databases of 18 states (so far). Eventually, all 50 states are expected to participate in this program. The Index System currently contains the genetic profiles of some 210,000 criminals and is expanding rapidly.[33] Although databases such as this one are crucial in terms of resolving criminal cases, the protection and integrity of stored samples remains a concern. There is a strong need for the safeguarding of DNA samples and the disclosure of DNA typing information. These safeguards must be precisely and clearly designed, standardized and responsibly implemented on either a state or national level. While some state legislators have addressed this issue – and legislation such as the Innocence Protection Act of 2000 have come into play –, very few laws exist to preserve evidence during a defendant's incarceration and arduous process of appeals.[34]

---

[32] See:" Innocence Project": "Causes and remedies of wrongful convictions," http://www.innocenceproject.org/causes/dna.php, Visited on Jan.24, 2003. "Larry Mayes was convicted of rape in Hammond, Ind., in 1982, based on an eyewitness identification by the victim and a primitive test of semen evidence that did not exclude him as the rapist. DNA testing had not been invented. In the summer of 2000, a law student volunteer, Resa Overhoudt, pressed Indiana authorities to locate the long-misplaced evidence kit. Tests showed that the rapist's DNA matched neither Mayes nor his alleged accomplice. The victim, it turned out, had been hypnotized before identifying Mayes as her attacker. "This one was a real eye-opener," says Fran Hardy, a criminal law professor at Indiana University-Indianapolis who oversaw the case. "It strongly suggests that single eyewitness identification cases should be problematic for all of us."

[33] See the U.S. Department of Justice, Office of Justice Programs, Bureau of Justice Statistic, Special Report http://www.ojp.usdoj.gov/bjs/glance/cxe.html.pdf, visited on Feb. 4, 2003.

[34] See Committee on DNA Technology in Forensic Science, Board on Biology, Commission on Life Sciences, National Research Council: "DNA Technology in Forensic Science," Chapter 5:"Forensic DNA Databanks and Privacy of Information," Pg. 115. (Washington, D.C. National Academy Press, 1992). "For example the Virginia law establishing a DNA profile databank for convicted offenders states that any person who, without authority, disseminates information

Another obstacle to the introduction of new evidence is timing. According to Barry Scheck, 33 states are restricting the time frame (within six months) to allow any claim of innocence based on new findings to be brought to the court. Only seven states permit the motion at any time.[35] But introducing DNA evidence in criminal cases (whether during or post trial) is just one element of a comprehensive approach in an effort, or rather, obvious need to "fix" the particular segment of the American criminal justice system in question – the application of capital punishment.

There are around 20,000 homicides in the United States each year. Thousands of criminals are sentenced to death. Few dispute the fact that many of the perpetrators of murder are, in fact, guilty. It is also true that few dispute the suggestion that there are cases wherein the courts fail. The Innocence Project has revealed a rather alarming statistic related to this conundrum: for every seven individuals executed, one innocent person is freed (it should be noted here that this figure includes all incarcerated prisoners, not just those confined to death row).[36] How is this possible? The answer requires a look at a range of contributing

---

contained in the databank shall be guilty of a Class 3 misdemeanor. Any person who disseminates, receives or otherwise uses or attempts to use information in the databank, knowing that such use is for purpose other than as authorized by law, shall be guilty of a Class. 1misdemeanor, except as authorized by law, any person who, for purposes of having DNA analysis performed, obtains or attempts to obtain any sample submitted to the Division of Forensic Science for analysis shall be guilty of a Class 5 felony." Also see: See The Justice Project, Campaign for criminal justice reform. http://www.justice.policy.net/ipa/#4, visited on Feb.4, 2003. "Senator Patrick Leahy (D-VT) sponsored SR 2690, Innocence Protection Act, to reduce the risk of executing innocent persons by ensuring that state and federal prisoners have access from to DNA testing. Unfortunately, there is no guarantee of access to testing, thresholds for access vary jurisdiction to jurisdiction, and there is often no requirement to preserve evidence."

[35] See Barry Scheck, Peter Neufeld and Jim Dwyer," Actual Innocence, When Justice Goes wrong and how to make it right," Chapter 11:"The Death of Innocents" Pg.282 (New York: A Signet Book, New American Library, 2000).

[36] See Dow, David R. and Mark Dow, with Foreword by Christopher Hitchens: "Machinery of Death, The Reality of America's Death penalty Regime," Part One: "How the Death Penalty really works," (New York and London, Routledge, 2002). Pg 12. Also See Scheck Barry, Peter Neufeld and Jim Dwyer, "Actual Innocence, When Justice Goes wrong and how to make it right," Chapter 11: "The Death of Innocents," Pg.282 (New York: A Signet Book, New American Library, 2000).

factors such as racial, political, and social biases, inept defense lawyers, mistaken eyewitnesses, and jailhouse snitches.[37]

There is an old saying: "Capital punishment means those without the capital get the punishment."[38] Most capital defendants are poor and therefore without a competent defense lawyer. Typically, they are represented by a court-appointed public defender. In jurisdictions that do not employ a public defender, indigent defendants are represented by lawyers that are simply unqualified, underpaid, and that lack sufficient funds for typical defense functions such as conducting independent investigations and hiring expert witnesses. Occasionally, these lawyers are nothing short of untrustworthy – many of these appointed advisors have already been disciplined by the American Bar Association.[39]

The following is a set of examples to illustrate how greatly an ineffective defense can influence the eventual result in a capital case – according to death penalty expert, David R. Dow:[40]

A lawyer who had never tried a capital case represented Harvey Duffy –a man on trial for his life –. The lawyer spent less than a day picking the jury – despite the fact that jury selection is perhaps the most critical phase of a capital murder trial. A qualified lawyer might have taken several weeks if not months to complete the same task. Another defendant was represented by counsel who, during his closing argument, said: "You are an extremely intelligent jury. You've got this man's life in your hands. You can take it or not. That's all I've got to

---

[37] See Garvey, Stephen P.:"Beyond Repair? America's Death Penalty," Chapter Three, by Ken Armstrong & Steve Mills: "Until I Can Be Sure": How the threat of Executing the Innocent Has Transformed the Death Penalty Debate, (Durham and London, Duke University Press, 2003). Pg 94-121. and Scheck, Barry, Peter Neufeld and Jim Dwyer," Actual Innocence, When Justice Goes wrong and how to make it Right," Chapters: 3 to 10(New York: A Signet Book, New American Library, 2000).

[38] See Rachel King: "Don't Kill in Our Names: Families of Murder Victims Speak Out Against the Death Penalty," Introduction, (Rutgers University Press, New Brunswick, New Jersey and London, 2003 Pg.3.

[39] Dow, David R. and Mark Dow, with Foreword by Christopher Hitchens: "Machinery of Death, The Reality of America's Death penalty Regime," Part One: "How the Death Penalty really works," (New York and London, Routledge, 2002). Pg 21. Pg.11-35. and quote Pg.21: "In many jurisdictions in the so called southern death belt, caps on fees that will be paid to lawyers representing capital defendants are astonishingly low. Counties in Georgia and Mississippi until recently set caps of $1000 in death penalty cases."

[40] Ibid. Biographies, Pg.289

say."[41] Even more bizarre was the case of a capital murder defendant that was represented by a lawyer that was having an affair with the defendant's wife. In the middle of the trial, the defendant was served with divorce papers. The lawyer and the defendant's wife were later married.[42] In another example – this one according to Barry Scheck – an attorney in Kentucky gave his business address as Kelly's Keg (a local watering hole). Scheck goes on to reveal that, in addition to having little to no experience, the lawyer literally missed the testimony of important witnesses because he was out of the courtroom, and (on at least one occasion) showed up for trial drunk. "When police searched his home, they found garbage bags hidden under a floor containing stolen property." Yet, "The court said that his behavior did not adversely affect his client."[43] Continuing along those same lines, a case in Texas tells of several defense attorneys sleeping through the majority of their respective trials. Similarly, "the court of criminal appeals in Texas refused relief to death row inmates represented by an attorney who slept at trial."[44]

The problem of inadequate legal representation and poor handling of a capital case was addressed in Senator Leahy's Innocence Protection Act of 2000.[45] The study showed that, according to the

---

[41] Ibid. Part One: "How the Death Penalty Really Works," Pg.22-23. Also see Robert Jay Lifton and Greg Mitchell, "Who Owns Death? Capital Punishment, the American conscience, and the end of executions," New York: Perennial, An Imprint of Harper Collins Publishers, 2000).

[42] Ibid.

[43] Scheck, Barry, Peter Neufeld and Jim Dwyer, "Actual Innocence, When Justice Goes wrong and how to make it right," Chapter Nine: "Sleeping Lawyers," (New York: A Signet Book, New American Library, 2000). Pg. 244

[44] See Garvey, Stephen P.: "Beyond Repair? America's Death Penalty," Chapter Three, by Ken Armstrong & Steve Mills: "Until I Can Be Sure: How the threat of Executing the Innocent Has Transformed the Death Penalty Debate," (Durham and London, Duke University Press, 2003). Pg.112.

[45] See: http://www.justice.policy.net/ipa/#4, visited on Feb.4, 2003. "U.S. Supreme Court Justice Sandra Day O'Connor, a life-long death penalty advocate, has expressed the need for better defense lawyers in death penalty cases. And Columbia University Law School Professor James Liebman's landmark study, A Broken System: Error Rates in Capital Cases found that quality of counsel was a leading cause of error. As with the DNA testing provision, the counsel provision has changed since the IPA's introduction. As introduced, the IPA would have established a commission to set national standards that states would be encouraged to adopt through funding 'carrots and sticks.' In the version that emerged from the Senate Judiciary Committee, the Department of Justice will make grants to states to establish or improve effective capital indigent defense systems. An effective system

American Bar Association, the legal standards for ineffective counsel employed by the courts are so low that, in most cases, the ABA has little or no power to sanction incompetent or inadequate lawyers.[46]

Many big cases rely on faulty testimony from jailhouse snitches that purposely lie (or are bought by cushy deals from the State), mistaken eyewitnesses, or coerced confessions. The testimony of jailhouse informants is little more than court-sanctioned hearsay. Typically, the testimony consists of conjecture by the informant that derives from a relayed conversation between another inmate and the accused. In return for their doctored (and often false) testimonies, snitches are typically granted a variety of benefits such as reduced sentences, access to personal luxuries while in prison, or even dropped charges. The testimony of an inmate was a key factor in the conviction of David Spence in Texas in 1984, leading to his execution in 1997:

> *"Spence was charged with murdering three teenagers in 1982. He was allegedly hired by a convenience store owner to kill another girl, and killed these victims by mistake. The convenience store owner, Muneer Deeb, was originally convicted and sentenced to death, but then was acquitted at a re-trial. The police lieutenant who supervised the investigation of Spence, Marvin Horton, later concluded: "I do not think David Spence committed this crime." Ramon Salinas, the homicide detective who actually conducted the investigation, said: "My opinion is that David Spence was innocent. Nothing from the investigation ever led us to any evidence that he was involved." No physical evidence connected Spence to the crime. The case against Spence was pursued by a zealous narcotics cop who relied on testimony of prison inmates who were granted favors in return for testimony."* [47]

---

includes a functionally independent entity to identify and appoint defense lawyers in capital cases, maintain a roster of qualified lawyers, conduct training, and ensure reasonable compensation at a rate comparable to the typical federal rate."

[46] See the American Bar Association, "Death Penalty Representation Project in 1986," http://www.abanet.org/deathpenalty/, visited on Feb.7, 2003.

[47] See: Death Penalty Information Center, Executed Despite Doubts About Guilt, http://www.deathpenaltyinfo.org/article.php? scid=6&did=111#executed, visited on May 23, 2005.

According to appellate rulings, the State is supposed to disclose to the US government any information concerning "deals" made with jailhouse informants – but prosecutors repeatedly fail to do so.[48]

When crime scenes do not offer biological evidence that can immediately implicate or exclude the suspect, the basis for conviction in a murder trial typically falls on the shoulders of eyewitness testimony. Too many cases unjustly rely upon the testimony of a single eyewitness. One such case is illustrated by the story of Gary Graham – executed by the state of Texas during George W. Bush's tenure as Governor. According to Dow, Gary Graham was convicted in the murder of Bobby Lambert based on testimony by one eyewitness. There was no forensic evidence to tie Graham to the shooting. Though lawyers submitted his case to dozens of state and federal courts, all of them refused to re-evaluate the clear evidence of innocence.[49]

> *"Fact showing that the single eyewitness upon whose testimony Graham was convicted was mistaken, and that Graham was innocent, were first discovered thereafter, in an investigation conducted within the first four months of 1993, nearly twelve years after Graham was convicted...His last appeal was refused on May 1, 2000. Shortly thereafter, an execution date of June 22, 2000, was set for Graham. He filed an original Habeas petition directly with the U.S. Supreme Court, but the Court denied review and a stay of execution by a 5 to 4 vote. Over waves of protests in Texas and around the country, Governor Bush and the Texas Board of Pardons and Paroles refused to intervene, and Graham was executed."*[50]

---

[48] See Garvey, Stephen P.: "Beyond Repair? America's Death Penalty," Chapter Three, by Ken Armstrong & Steve Mills: "Until I Can Be Sure": How the threat of Executing the Innocent Has Transformed the Death Penalty Debate, (Durham and London, Duke University Press, 2003). Pg.106-197.

[49] See Dow, David R. and Mark Dow, with Foreword by Christopher Hitchens: "Machinery of Death, The Reality of America's Death penalty Regime," Chapter Seven, by Mandy Welch and Richard Burr: "The Politics of finality and the execution of the innocent; the case of Gary Graham," (New York and London, Routledge, 2002). Pg 127-143.

[50] Ibid Pg 141.

The case of Joseph O'Dell, who was convicted in 1986 in Virginia and executed in 1997 is yet another example of the swift, dubious, and irreversible justice in America:

> "New DNA blood evidence has thrown considerable doubt on the murder and rape conviction of O'Dell. In reviewing his case in 1991, three Supreme Court Justices, said they had doubts about O'Dell's guilt and whether he should have been allowed to represent himself. Without the blood evidence, there is little linking O'Dell to the crime. In September 1996, the 4th Circuit of the U.S. Court of Appeals reinstated his death sentence and upheld his conviction. The U.S. Supreme Court refused to review O'Dell's claims of innocence and held that its decision regarding juries being told about the alternative sentence of life-without-parole was not retroactive to his case. O'Dell asked the state to conduct DNA tests on other pieces of evidence to demonstrate his innocence but was refused. He was executed on July 23rd."[51]

With all the aforementioned in mind, it simply cannot be disputed that the American justice system is sentencing innocent people to death. The exact number of innocent people executed by the State is difficult to determine, however, because of all the obstacles in the way of proving innocence post-mortem. According to the executive director of the DPIC, Richard Dieter, "You can't appeal to a court anymore, and the attorneys are busy with other cases. The only possibility would be if the state would admit to having committed an error – which it hardly ever does."[52]

To date, 159 wrongfully convicted people have been exonerated.[53] All of them were innocent, yet were sitting on death row, awaiting a firing squad, electrocution, or lethal injection for crimes they did not commit. At the same time, the majority (if not all) of the actual perpetrators in these 159 crimes have gone unpunished.

---

[51] See: Death Penalty Information Center, Executed Despite Doubts About Guilt, http://www.deathpenaltyinfo.org/article.php?scid=6&did=111#executed, visited on May 23, 2005

[52] See, Canadian Coalition Against the Death Penalty, http://ccadp.org/nathanielbarley.htm, visited on June 9, 2005.

[53] See The Innocence Project, http://www.innocenceproject.org/, visited on June 2, 2005.

Some argue that the discovery of the innocence of a death row inmate actually proves that the system works. This argument serves only to confirm the impression that American justice routinely operates by twisting the facts. It fails to grasp the significance of human life or even the overwhelming responsibility that must fall to the State whenever a life is at stake.

The possibility to execute an innocent person is a strong argument for abolition of the death penalty. More horrifying however, is the fact that the execution of innocent people seems to have had little or no impact on American opinion about capital punishment. As it now stands, it is highly unlikely that America will abolish the death penalty anytime soon.[54] In the meantime, however, prohibition of executions in cases that are decided on witness testimony alone – whether by one witness, a jailhouse snitch, or forced confession – would perhaps afford some consolation and hope for the condemned people. Every society has the right to protect itself from criminal activity and murder. Nevertheless, is the death penalty even effective in curbing said criminal activity? The answer to this question is a resounding "no". The reality is that – despite the presence of this most heinous of punishments – criminals continue to commit murder at a steady rate. To justify the death penalty with the argument that it works to discourage and even preempt the crime is pure folly. Many criminologists do not believe that the death penalty is a particularly effective deterrent:

> *...in study after study during the first six decades of this century scholars documented that murder rates were often higher in death penalty than in abolitionist jurisdictions, and that abolition and/or reintroduction of capital punishment was sometimes followed by an increase in murders and sometimes not. Based on this evidence, most criminologists came to agree with Sellin that: "the presence of the death penalty in law and practice has no discernible effect as a deterrent to murder.*[55]

---

[54] See Stuart Banner: "The Death Penalty: An American History," Epilogue, (Cambridge: Harvard University Press, 2002). Pg 307-314.
[55] See James R. Acka, Robert M. Bohm, Charls S.Lanier, "America's Experiment with Capital Punishment," 2nd.ed. Carolina Academic Press, Durham, North Carolina, 2003, Chapter Eight: "Is Capital Punishment an Effective Deterrent for Murder? An Examination of Social Science Research," by Buth D. Peterson, William C. Bailey, Pg. 253.

A case can be made for the argument that the existence and acceptance of *lex talions* or "a life for a life"[56] is little more than simple vengeance on the part of the government and the members of the victims' families. Although it is true that some members of the victims' families express a lack of rest or "closure" that is often quelled by the execution of the murderer in question, the following excerpt from a speech by Coretta Scott King, presented before the National Coalition suggests that there are differing opinions:

As one whose husband and mother-in-law have died the victims of murder assassination, I stand firmly an unequivocally opposed to the death penalty for those convicted of capital offenses. An evil deed is not redeemed by an evil deed of retaliation. Justice is never advanced in the taking of a human life. Morality is never upheld by a legalized murder.[57]

The American justice system does not look favorably upon a victim's family members who oppose the death penalty. "Sometimes the justice system shuns them: prosecutors, parole boards, and judges have silenced people who have tried to speak against the death penalty."[58]

As is traditionally understood, the right to life is natural, universal and non-transferable. Capital punishment, therefore, seems to defy tradition. The practice should be considered unacceptable in the eyes of any civilized and advanced nation – in particular, democratic nations such as the U.S.; self-proclaimed guardian of human rights worldwide.

Whether State-sponsored or otherwise, the majority of those polled indicate that the human right to life is sacrosanct. Weighing the pros and cons of capital punishment – and, indeed, its very existence in this country – is a process greatly perverted by politics. In many states, the death penalty has been perpetuated simply because judges and prosecutors saw it as a vehicle for reelection. Executions grab headlines – and headlines are consistently the most favorable element to winning

---

[56] See Hugo Adam Bedau, (1984) Publications and information resource of the American Civil Liberties Union National Office, Speech to the National Coalition to Abolish the Death Penalty, Washington D.C. September 26.
[57] Ibid.
[58] See Rachel King: "Don't Kill in Our Names: Families of Murder Victims Speak Out Against the Death Penalty," Introduction, (Rutgers University Press, New Brunswick, New Jersey and London, 2003 Pg.1.

office.⁵⁹ Oftentimes, the merits of an individual case are largely ignored during election years.

Death sentence statistics in America reveal that a significant discrepancy exists between the numbers of sentenced and executed minorities (particularly blacks and latinos) and whites. For example, according to two of the country's foremost researchers on race and capital punishment, law professor David Baldus, statistician George Woodworth, and other professors in Philadelphia have concluded that, "the odds of receiving a death sentence (in this particular state – Philadelphia) are nearly four times higher if the defendant is black." [60] The same source also states the following:

These results were obtained after analyzing and controlling fore case differences such as the severity of the crime and the background of the defendant. The data were subjected to various forms of analysis, but the conclusion was clear: blacks were being sentenced to death far in excess of other defendants for similar crimes.*[61]*

Another study conducted by Professor Jeffrey Pokorak and researchers at St. Mary's University Law School in Texas offered some explanation for why the application of the death penalty remains racially bias. Their study found that the key decision makers in the death penalty cases around the country are almost exclusively white men. Of the chief District Attorneys in counties applying the death penalty in the United States, nearly 98% are white and only 1% are African-American".[62]

The death penalty is a "direct descendant of lynching and other forms of racial violence and racial oppression in America."[63] This is

---

[59] See: Illinois Coalition against The Death Penalty, "What's wrong with the Death Penalty?" http://www.icadp.org/Pg.17.html, visited on January 9,2003.

[60] See: Death Penalty Information Center, "The Death Penalty in Black and White: Who Lives, Who Dies, Who Decides" – "Executive Summary", by Richard C. Deither, Esq. Executive Director, Death Penalty Information Centre, June 1998. http://www.deathpenaltyinfo.org/article.php?scid=45&did=539#Executive%20Summary, visited on August 8,2005.

[61] Ibid.

[62] Ibid.

[63] See Dow, David R. and Mark Dow, with Foreword by Christopher Hitchens: "Machinery of Death, the Reality of America's Death penalty Regime," Chapter Three, by Stephen B. Bright: "Discrimination, Death and Denial: Race and the Death Penalty," (New York and London, Routledge, 2002). Pg 45-48. Also see Stephen P. Garvey: "Beyond Repair? America's Death Penalty," Chapter Four by

perhaps one of the last remaining frontiers for the Equal Rights movement – equality in capital cases. The following is an excerpt from a speech concerning the Federal Death Penalty Abolition Act of 1999 delivered by Senator Russell Feingold to the U.S. Congress:

> *"Another reason we need to abolish the death penalty is the specter of racism in our criminal justice system. Even though our nation has abandoned slavery and segregation, we unfortunately are still living with vestiges of institutional racism. In some cases, racism can be found at every stage of a capital trial – in the selection of the jurors, during the presentation of evidence, and sometimes during the jury deliberations."* [64]

To illustrate another example of racial discrimination in the American courtroom, consider the case of Wilburn Dobbs. In a mere three days, Dobbs was convicted and sentenced to death in Georgia for the murder of a white man. The unprecedented and outrageous attitude of Dobbs' court-appointed lawyer toward African Americans is described by the federal district court as follows:

> *Dobbs' trial attorney was outspoken about his views. He said that many blacks are uneducated and would not make good teachers, but do make good basketball players. He opined that blacks are less educated and less intelligent than whites either because of their nature or because 'my granddaddy had slaves.' He said that integration has led to deteriorating neighborhoods and schools are referred to in the black community in Chattanooga as "black boy jungle." He*

Shery Lynn Johnson: "Race and Capital Punishment," (Durham and London, Duke University Press, 2003). "There is no question that the death penalty in this country historically was sought and imposed in a racially discriminatory manner. The "distorting effect of racial discrimination" in the administration of the death penalty ate in truth as old as our Republic. The long history of the relation between race and capital cases has been painstakingly documented elsewhere." Pg.123.

[64] See Congressional Record, Proceedings and Debates of the 106th Congress, Second Session, Vol.146, Washington, Tuesday, November 16, 2000, Nos. 163, "The Federal Death Penalty Abolition Act of 1999," http://www.senate.gov/~feingold/speeches/senflor/abolitionspeech.html, visited on Feb.28, 2003.

strongly implied that blacks have inferior morals by relating a story about sex in a classroom. He also said that, when he was young, a maid was hired with the understanding that she would steal some items. He said that blacks in Chattanooga are more troublesome than blacks in Walker County [Georgia]... The attorney stated that he uses the word 'nigger' jokingly.[65]

As long as this kind of behavior in the courtrooms across the United States goes unpunished (and, in fact, is silently accepted and condoned), it is unlikely for discrimination and racial prejudice to diminish. The American people are aware of the formal norm of equality but in many cases, fail to practice it.[66]

Despite the overwhelming evidence of the persistence of prejudice against minorities in the American criminal justice system, authorities strongly deny that the use of the death penalty is in any way influenced by racial bias. The refusal to admit and address obvious racial discrimination in the administration of capital punishment is yet another proof of how serious this problem has become. Accordingly, it is much more convenient for the authorities to turn a blind eye and constantly deny the obvious. In other words: "Legislators on both the federal and the state level have failed to pass civil right laws regarding the death penalty for fear of stopping capital punishment entirely."[67]

Considering the widespread recognition (and even the acknowledgment) of the problems in the U.S. criminal justice system, it seems both necessary and wise for the American government to consider and continue to explore all avenues for reform (if not abolishment) of capital punishment. With every execution, American society only deepens its culture of violence which, in turn, only serves to support a global impression that: "The United States is one of the most violent democratic countries in the world ...also the only Western

---

[65] See Dow, David R. and Mark Dow, with Foreword by Christopher Hitchens: "Machinery of Death, the Reality of America's Death penalty Regime," Chapter Three, Pg.48. (New York and London, Routledge, 2002).

[66] See Garvey, Stephen P. "Beyond Repair? America's Death Penalty," Chapter Four by Shery Lynn Johnson: "Race and Capital Punishment," (Durham and London, Duke University Press, 2003). Pg.143.

[67] See: Death Penalty Information Center," The Death Penalty in Black and White: Who Lives, Who Dies, Who Decides" – "Executive Summary", by Richard C. Deither, Esq. Executive Director, Death Penalty Information Centre, June 1998. http://www.deathpenaltyinfo.org/article.php?scid=45&did=539#Executive%20Summary, visited on August 8,2005.

democracy that uses the death penalty."[68] In order to understand why Americans are comfortable with violence, the following chapter of this paper will proceed to discuss several facets of the fundamental values rooted within American culture. It will go on to highlight the key differences between the U.S. and its closest democratic neighbor, Canada – along with several other well-developed Western nations – concerning the issue of capital punishment.

---

[68] See Rachel King: "Don't Kill in Our Names," Families of Murder Victims Speak Out Against the Death Penalty," Afterward, (Rutgers University Press, New Brunswick, New Jersey and London, 2003), Pg.275.

Chapter Two

The American vs. the International Stance on Capital Punishment

The distinction between the views held by American/Canadian society and Western European nations regarding the death penalty

No nation or society is based on a single, enduring set of values. Every culture is a quilt of multiple values, at least some of which appear to contradict others. [69] Further, there is indissoluble interaction between the political system and culture. In other words, culture influences the system and the system affects culture in its turn. Thus, culture incorporates all the influences: historical, religious, ethnic, political that affect a society's values and attitudes. Yet, political culture generally refers to the collective opinions, attitudes and values of individuals about politics.[70]

The traditional concept of political culture in the U.S. and Canada is similar to the conditions listed above. Democracy is the dominant value expressed by both countries. The preamble to the Canadian Charter of Rights and Freedoms and the American Bill of Rights

---

[69] Uslaner, Eric M. "The Decline of Comity in Congress," Chapter 4: "Values, Norms, and Society," (Ann Arbor: The University of Michigan Press, 1993), Pg. 63.

[70] See Mattei Dogan and Domenique Pelassy, "How to Compare Nations, Strategies in Comparative Politics," sec. ed. Chapter 8: "Political Culture: From Nation to Nation," (Chatham, New Jersey: Chatham House Publishers, Inc. 1990), Pg. 68-77.

acknowledges a commitment to promote a free and democratic society.[71] Furthermore, popular sovereignty allows people in both societies to have the proverbial final say – which, in large part, is voiced via the election process, held at specific intervals. In addition, political equality is represented by the idea that all citizens are equal – a concept that is given physical form through the notion of one person, one vote.[72] If one looks beyond the consensus of democracy, however – according to Lipset's analysis, *Continental Divide* – differences between American and Canadian values become more apparent.

The creation of the United States was based on revolutionary origins while, in Canada, those origins were influenced by a counter-revolutionary ideology. According to Lipset, the true difference between US and Canadian roots is as follows: "Canada has been and is a more class-aware, elitist, law-abiding, statist, collectively oriented, and particularistic (group-oriented society) than the United States."[73] Moreover, the U.S. remains the world's last stronghold of individualism while Canada boasts a long-standing tradition as an organic community in which all people are aware of their place and do their respective part to contribute to the welfare of the whole.[74] The Canadian political tradition has maintained a strong policy of multiculturalism and the recognition of the rights of outside groups. Lipset acknowledges that a similar ethnic revival has occurred in the U.S. – a country that has seen the analogy of the melting pot evolve steadily into that of the mosaic.[75]

Another fine line between American and Canadian ideals falls between populism and elitism. Populism is the belief that the will of the people should dominate a country's elite. The word of the many outweighs the word of the few – however wealthy, powerful, and influential the few may be.

---

[71] See Heineman, Robert A., Steven A. Peterson and Thomas H. Rasmussen, "American Government," (New York, Toronto: McGraw-Hill Book Company, 1989); also see Earl H. Fry, "Canadian Government and Politics in Comparative Perspective," (Lanham, MD: University Press America,, 1984).

[72] Ibid. See also R.D. Olling and M.W. Westmacott, "Perspective on Canadian Federalism," (Scarborough, Ontario: Prentice Hall, Canada, 1988).

[73] See Seymour Martin Lipset, "Continental Divide, The Values and institutions of the United States and Canada," (New York: Routledge, 1990), Pg.8.

[74] Ibid. Also see Eric M. Uslaner, "The Decline of Comity in Congress," Chapter 4: "Values, Norms, and Society," (Ann Arbor: The University of Michigan Press, 1993), Pg. 63-102.

[75] See Seymour Martin Lipset, "Continental Divide, the Values and Institutions of the United States and Canada," (New York, London: Routledge, 1990).

> *In strictly historical terms, Populism refers to a third-party movement that materialized in America in the 1890s, generating a spirited energy that also caused a certain alarm near the seats of the mighty. The Populists engaged in a social analysis of contemporary American society that yielded a range of proposed economic reforms. Foremost among them was the Subtreasury Land and Loan System, which re conceptualized American banking and proposed a restructured monetary system that would fundamentally alter the power relationships between bankers and everyone else. The Populist concern about "concentrated capital" extended beyond banks to include large-scale business organizations generally. Populist reformers felt that business domination of the political process--through massive campaign contributions to friendly officeholders and persistently effective lobbying in the national Congress and the state legislatures--had proceeded to the point that the practice had begun to undermine the democratic idea itself."*[76]

In addition, American ideology, according to Lipset, can be described in five words: "liberty, egalitarianism, individualism, populism, and laissez-faire". The revolutionary ideology, as Lipset further explains, is liberalism of 18th and 19th century meaning," as distinct from conservative Toryism, statist communitarianism, mercantilism, and noblesse oblige dominant in monarchical, state-church formed cultures."[77] It is important to note here that comparing the nations is never an easy task nor that the conclusions drown from that comparison are absolutes. The following is the example offered by Lipset that states: "when Canada is evaluated by reference to the United States, it appears as more elitist. Law-abiding, and statist, but when considering the variations between Canada and Britain, Canada looks more anti-statist, violent and egalitarian."[78] Canada does not have the system of checks and balances as in the U.S. and members of the Canadian senate, judiciary and local commissions are appointed.

---

[76] See: Answers.com, American History, Populism:
http://www.answers.com/topic/populism, visited on August 4, 2005.
[77] See Seymour Martin Lipset, "American Exceptionalism, A Double–Edged Sword,"Chapter1:"Ideology, Politics, and Deviance", (New York&London, W.W. Northon &Company, 1997), Pg.31.
[78] Ibid. Pg.33.

Canada is a multiparty system in which one party usually dominates; liberalism, toryism and socialism are three distinct ideological approaches to politics; balance among them is strongly in favor of liberalism. The Liberal Party, the Conservative Party and the New Democratic Party, have been represented in every Parliament since 1935.[79]

General ideas of the structure and functions of the U.S. government are provided by their Constitution. Federalism and the separation of powers, two major political parties, heavy influence from special interest groups and the mass media, protection of property and individual rights.[80]

Despite their many similarities, one key issue in which Canadian and American societies fundamentally differ is that of the death penalty. Capital punishment was removed from Canadian criminal code in 1976 and replaced with a mandatory 25-year prison sentence without parole. Capital punishment was retained for a number of military offenses under the National Defense Act of 1950, however. The death penalty could be imposed only if the verdict was unanimous and the execution could be carried out only if approved by the Governor General in Council. Officially, an execution in Canada was by firing squad – but, during the span of the Act, no executions were carried out. In 1998, Canada abolished the death penalty for all crimes.[81]

Coincidentally, in 1976, capital punishment was reinstated in the U.S. – and, to date, it is practiced in 38 American states. All 37 death penalty states employ lethal injection as their method of execution.[82]

---

[79] See Donald J. Savoie, "Governing from the Centre, The Concentration of Power in Canadian Politics," (Toronto, Buffalo, London: University of Toronto Press, 1999). Also see "About Government, Political Parties," http://canada.gc.ca/main_e.html, visited on April 7, 2003.

[80] See Herman Charles Pritchett: "The American Constitutional System," 2nd ed. (New York: McGraw Hill, 1967). See Jeffrey M. Stonecash, Mark d. Brewer & Mack D. Mariani: "Diverging Parties, Social change, Realignment, and Party Polarization," (Cambridge and Oxford, Westview Press, 2003).

[81] See David. B. Chandler, "Capital Punishment in Canada, A Sociological Study of Repressive Law," The Carleton Library No.94. Published by McClelland and Stewart Limited in association with the Institute of Canadian Studies, Carleton University, 1976). Also see Amnesty International, "When the State Kills, The death penalty: a human rights issue," "The death penalty worldwide, Canada," (New York Amnesty International USA, 1989). Pg116.

[82] See Death Penalty Information Centre, Methods of Execution, Until 2002, state of Alabama, had the electric chair as a mandatory method of execution. "Legislation that changes the primary method of execution in Alabama from the electric chair to

The European Union is conducting an international campaign against capital punishment and it has made the abolition of the death penalty a condition for membership. In other words, if the country wants to become a member of the European Union, one of the requirements for membership is to abolish the death penalty. Furthermore, the European Union has also modified its extradition laws, now refusing to extradite convicts to the U.S. when the charges against them carry the death penalty. According to the DPIC report:

> *"In addition to the execution of foreign nationals, there are numerous instances where people wanted for crime in the U.S. are arrested in other countries. The question of extradition and the possible use of the death penalty have risen major concerns throughout Europe, Canada, Mexico, and parts of Africa. The urgency of this issue has been heightened by the events of Sept. 11 and the war on terrorism. Suspected terrorists not only may face the death penalty in the U.S. if extradited, but they may also be tried in a military tribunal that lacks the normal due process afforded defendants in the civilian courts. While the U.S. sorely wants to bring such suspects to justice, many countries just as strongly believe that the death penalty is a human rights issue and extradition in such circumstances would be a violation of deeply held principles"* . . . [83]

---

lethal injection was signed by Governor Donald Siegelman on April 25. As of July 1, 2002, lethal injection will be used as the method of execution unless an inmate requests the electric chair." Also see Appendix A in Appendices. Also see Death penalty Information Centre, State by state Death Penalty Information- States With the Death Penalty,
http://deathpenaltyinfo.org, visited on May 2, 2003. Also see Amnesty International, "When the State Kills: The Death Penalty: a Human Rights Issue," "The Death Penalty Worldwide, The United States of America," (New York: Amnesty International USA, 1989). Pg. 227.

[83] See Death Penalty Information Center, Countries that have been abolished the death penalty since 1976.
http://www.deathpenaltyinfo.org/article.php?scid=30&did=140#1976, Visited on April 8, 2003.Also see:
http://www.deathpenaltyinfo.org/article.php?scid=17&did=806,"International Influence on the Death Penalty in the U.S.", by Richard C. Dieter, Executive Director of the Death Penalty information Centre, From: Foreign Service Journal, October 2003. visited on August 9, 2005.

In such politically similar societies, why the stark dichotomy between U.S. and Canadian/Western European views on the application of capital punishment? The simplest answer to this question may seem to be the sociological observation that the United States, during the 60's and 70's, had a much higher homicide rate than that of any other Western industrialized nation. Although the rate dropped slightly in the early 1980's, it was again high later in the decade. As of the 1990s, the U.S. homicide rate was four and a half times that of Canada, nine times that of France or Germany, and 13 times that of the United Kingdom.[84]

The general claim that the crime policy is determined primarily by crime rate is analyzed in the study of comparative non-capital penal policies. The study posits that – crime rates aside – death penalty countries such as the U.S. possess certain other fundamental characteristics that contribute to their propensity to impose capital punishment. Atop the list (especially in America) are morality, history, and politics.[85]

Another argument to explain the discrepancy points to collective vs. individual responsibility. According to Shipman, American views on responsibility tend to be more individualistic – with the focus placed on the need to punish the guilty party. In Europe, the view is generally more collective or societal – this is to say, the emphasis is on how and why the society or community failed by facilitating such horrible crimes.[86]

Some detractors to abolition of the death penalty would suggest that repealing capital punishment in the U.S. would result in an even higher murder rate. This argument is refuted by a careful study of Canada's murder rate from 1976 to the present. Despite overturning the death penalty in 1976, the homicide rate in Canada did not increase. In fact, Statistics Canada reports that the murder rate for 2001 remained stable for the third year in a row at approximately 1.8 homicides for every 100,000 population.[87] The total number of murders in Canada in 2001 was 554, just eight more than in 2000, but 167 fewer than in

---

[84] See Michael Tonry and Richard S. Frase, "Sentencing and Sanctions in Western Countries, "Punishment, Policies and Patterns in Western Countries," (New York: Oxford University Press, 2001), Pg.13.

[85] See Michael Tonry and Richard S. Frase, "Sentencing and Sanctions in Western Countries, "Punishment, Policies and Patterns in Western Countries," (New York: Oxford University Press, 2001), Pg. 7-18.

[86] See Marlin Shipman, "The Penalty is Death, U.S. Newspaper Coverage of Women's Executions," Epilog, (Columbia and London: University of Missouri Press, 2002), Pg.305.

[87] See Statistic Canada, "Justice and Crime, Homicide rate," http://www.statcan.ca/english/Pgdb/legal01.htm, visited on April 8, 2003.

1975, the year before capital punishment was abolished. Figure 1.2. illustrates an incredibly low murder rate in Canada in 1999. During that same year, the U.S. homicide rate was 5.7 per 100,000 populations (according to the U.S. Bureau of Justice Statistics) – nearly three times greater than that of Canada.[88]

Figure 1.1. Source: Statistics Canada, April 8, 2003.

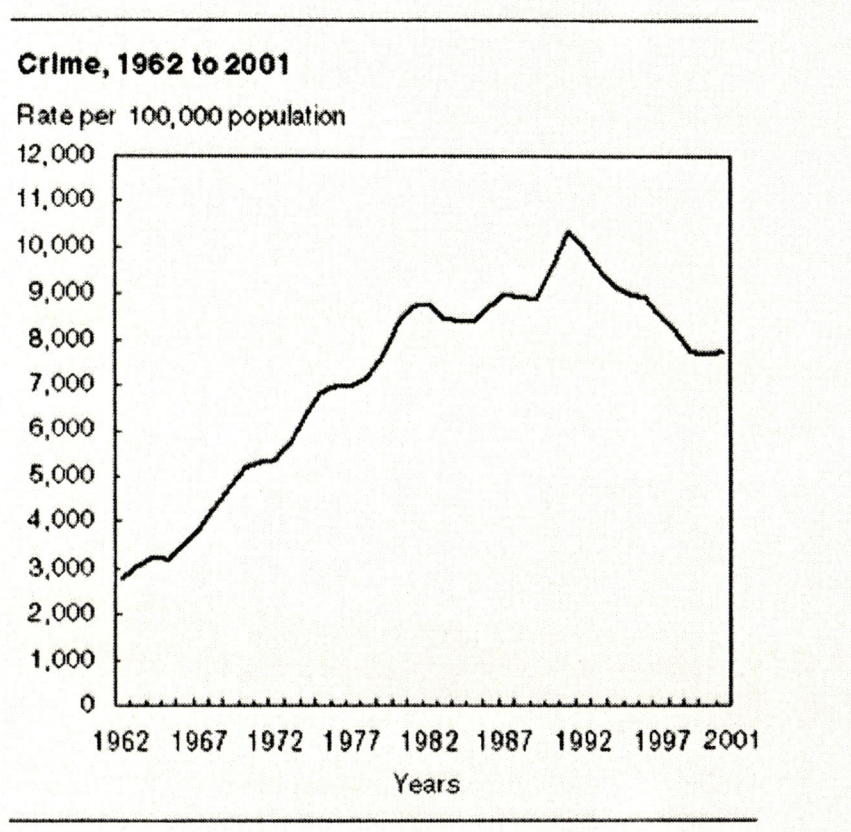

Politically, gun control is one of the few issues on which Republicans and Democrats dramatically disagree. Most Democrats favor tighter gun laws while the majority of Republicans are opposed to any new legislation, saying the problem lies in the enforcement of

---

[88] See U.S. Department of Justice, Office of Justice Programs, Bureau of Justice Statistics Publications, http://www.ojp.usdoj.gov/bjs/pubalp2.htm, visited on April 8.2003.

existing laws.[89] American public opinion is also sharply divided between those calling for tighter controls and those that insist on the right to bear arms. According to ABC News, gun control advocates often point out that countries with lower firearm ownership than the U.S. have fewer homicides and firearm-related deaths. However, the fact is that most of these countries had a much lower firearm homicide rate even before gun control legislation was enacted.[90]

Just 39% of Americans trust the Democrats to handle gun control, while 31% prefer the Republicans and an unusually large number, 22%, do not trust either party. Support for stricter gun control laws is much higher among women (80%) than men (54%). 66% of people who own guns support mandatory trigger locks, background checks, and a ban on mail order or Internet gun sales – as illustrated by Figure 2.2.[91]

Figure 2.2.

Opinions on Gun Issues

	Support		Oppose	
	Total	% Strong*	Total	% Strong*
Stricter gun control	67	82	31	68
Background checks at gun shows	89	87	11	64
Ban on assault weapons	79	85	19	63
Mandatory trigger locks	75	81	22	64
Ban on mail order and Internet gun sales	70	86	28	68

*Percentage of total who say they feel that way "strongly."

Source: ABCNEWS. Com. May 2, 2003[92]

---

[89] See Washington post, Nation, Gun Control, http://www.washingtonpost.com/wp-dyn/nation/specials/socialpolicy/guncontrol/, March 7, 2003.
[90] See: ABC News, Opinions on Gun Issues, http://abcnews.go.com/sections/us/DailyNews/guns_poll990518.html, May 2, 2003.
[91] Ibid.
[92] See ABC News, Opinions on Gun Issues, http://abcnews.go.com/sections/us/DailyNews/guns_poll990518.html, May 2, 2003.

The most powerful proponent of the right to bear arms is the National Rifle Association (NRA). The group considers gun ownership to be a basic right protected by the second Amendment. The Amendment reads as follows: "A well regulated militia, being necessary to the security of a Free State, the right of the people to keep and bear arms shall not be infringed." [93]

Advocates of gun control (the major opposition to the NRA) succeeded in passing two laws in 1994. The Brady Law requires background checks for purchasing a gun and the Violent Crime and Control Act (signed into law by President Clinton) represented the first federal Assault Weapons Ban, preventing the future manufacture and import of military-style assault weapons.[94] Despite these landmark changes, the controversy over gun ownership and the connection between the accessibility of weapons and violence remains the same..[95]

Gun control is perhaps the least of the influences on American policy when it comes to the issue of capital punishment, however. The central tenant that separates American ideology and culture from that of other Western countries is perhaps best described in the following lines:

> *"What makes American culture relatively distinctive is that it is a society which places a high premium on economic affluence and social ascent for all its members... This leads naturally to the subsidiary theme that success or failure are results wholly of personal qualities, that he who fails has only himself to blame, for the corollary to the concept of the self-made man and self-unmade man. To the extent that this cultural definition is assimilated by those who have not maid their mark, failure represents a double defeat: the manifest*

---

[93] Wilson Q. James, "American Government, Brief Version," Sec. ed. Appendix:"The Constitution of the United States – Amendment II," Pg. A13. (Lexington, Massachusetts, Toronto: D.C. Health and Company, 1990).

[94] See Brady Campaign and the Brady Center to Prevent Gun violence, http://www.bradycampaign.org/about/index.asp, "The Brady Law was named for James Brady, the Presidential press secretary who was shot and paralyzed in a 1981 assassination attempt on Ronald Reagan. In 1993, Congress passed the Brady law, which requires background checks to prohibit gun sales to criminals and others, including those with a history of mental illness. Since the law went into effect in February 1994, background checks have stopped more than 600,000 gun sales to prohibited purchasers; thousands of lives were saved." visited on March 4, 2003.

[95] See article "Dealers in Death" by Nina Planck, Magazine "Time" Canadian edition, November 2, 1998, Pg 34- 36.

defeat of remaining far behind in the race for success and the implicit defeat of not having the capacities and moral stamina needed for success... It is in this cultural setting that, in a significant portion of cases, the threat of defeat motivates me to the use of those tactics, beyond the law or the mores, which promise "success".".[96](Lipset quoted a sociologist: R. Merton)

In other words, Americans are much more likely to be concerned with the success as the final result than with the ways and means in achieving that success [97]

Political equality, political freedom and majority rule are the basics of a political identity formulated around values set down by the American Declaration of Independence.[98] In addition, many still pursue the "American Dream"[99] – a seemingly inherent yearning for individual opportunity, justice, and success. The U.S. also seems to believe that they are destined to control the world's affairs – noteworthy here is that they are probably the most vocal proponents of international human rights.

The death penalty is viewed as a violation of human rights and the International Human Rights Law but Americans openly disregard and consistently refuse to be bound by international human rights treaties in its own practice until 1992 – when the Senate finally ratified the International Convent on Civil and Political Rights – but, strangely enough, not the International Convent on Economic, Social, and Cultural Rights.[100] Moreover, despite two World Wars, the Holocaust,

---

[96] See Seymour Martin Lipset, "American Exceptionalism, A Double–Edged Sword,"Chapter1:"Ideology, Politics, and Deviance", (New York&London, W.W. Northon &Company, 1997). Pg. 47.

[97] Ibid.

[98] See Herman Charles Pritchett: "The American constitutional system," 2nd.ed. (New York: McGraw Hill, 1967). See Jeffrey M. Stonecash, Mark d. Brewer & Mack D. Mariani: "Diverging Parties, Social Change, Realignment, and Party Polarization," (Cambridge and Oxford, Westview Press, 2003).

[99] See Jeffrey Simpson: "Star-Spangled Canadian," (Toronto: Harper Collins, 2000) and Robert Putnam: "Bowling Alone," (New York: Simon and Schuster, 2000).

[100] See "International Human Rights," (Dilemmas in World Politics), Second Edition, by Jack Donnelly, Chapter One: "Human Rights as an Issue in World Politics," Pg.15, (Colorado: University of Denver, Westview Press, A Member of the Perseus Book Group, 15, 1999. See Amnesty International: "United States of America: The Death Penalty," (London: Amnesty International Publications, 1987) *and* Amnesty International: "The Machinery of Death: A Shocking Indictment of Capital Punishment in the United States," (New York: Amnesty International USA, 1995). Also see: "Like Water on Stone," The story of Amnesty International, Chapter 9: The USA – Land of Free? (London: Allen Lane The Penguin Press, 2001)."The

the Japanese attack on Pearl Harbor, the atomic bomb, the Civil Rights movement, Vietnam, Watergate and other affairs, America's view of itself remains fundamentally unchanged. They view themselves as a chosen, rather "exceptional" people on mission to protect human rights and promote democracy around the world by exporting their values and by overthrowing legitimate governments and setting up puppet regimes to make sure that the U.S. interests are safe and protected. (as, for example, in the Middle East, Africa, and Latin America).[101]

The promotion of democracy is perhaps a noble cause but, in Lowenthal's words: "The United States should never pretend that it can promote democracy abroad by trampling upon it at home."[102] Indeed, if one takes into account the highly publicized and tragic incident that was the Waco, Texas fiasco – when the Bureau of Alcohol, Tobacco and Firearms raided the compound of a religious group known as the Branch Davidians[103] – one may conclude that the protection of human rights in America is applied from case to case. In other words, America's well-established democracy, with all its rights and freedoms, sometimes denies those rights and freedoms when they apply to specific groups of people that challenge the status quo.

USA was founded in the name of democracy, political and legal equality, and individual freedom. However, despite its claims to international leadership in the field of human rights, and its many institutions to protect individual civil liberties, it is failing to deliver the fundamental promise of rights for all."Pg.253.

[101] Ibid. Chapter Five: "Human Rights and Foreign Policy," Pg 87. Exceptionalism is, "the belief that the United States is different from (and generally superior to) most other countries." Also see "Exporting Democracy, The United States and Latin America," Case Studies, edited by Abraham F. Lowenthal, (Baltimore and London: The Johns Hopkins University Press, 1991), Chapter 9:"The Imposition of Democracy" by Laurence Whitehead and Chapter 10: "The United States and Latin American Democracy: Learning from History" by Abraham F. Lowenthal.

[102] "Exporting Democracy, The United States and Latin America," Case Studies, edited by Abraham F.Lowenthal, (Baltimore and London: The Johns Hopkins University Press, 1991), Chapter 10: "The United States and Latin American Democracy: Learning from History" by Abraham F. Lowenthal, Pg.282.

[103] See Richard Abanes: "American Militias, Rebelion, Rasizm and Religion," foreword by Roy Innis, Chairman, Congress of Racial Equality (C.O.R.E.) (Downers Grove, Illinois: Intervarsity Press1996), Pg. 50. Tobacco and Firearms (ATF) planned a raid on the compound of a religious group, the Branch Davidians, which was supposedly harboring weapons; the raid failed and resulted in the deaths of four federal agents. A fifty-one day standoff ended when federal agents tried to take the compound. In the fire that broke out, more then eighty members of the sect, including two dozen children, were killed.

Violence is deeply rooted and silently accepted in American society and has become a lifestyle or an adopted strategy for solving a variety of conflicts. Violence is everywhere; in video games, movies, music, and the Internet. Newscasts do their fair share to feed the public's appetite for violence, as well. Under the guise of the public's "right to know," the media too often glamorizes violent acts through sensational headlines and endlessly repeated coverage in a deplorable attempt to boost ratings. Research suggests that the youth in America spend 38 hours each week viewing unsupervised television. On average, they witness over 200,000 acts of violence on television – including 16,000 murders – before age 18.[104] Although it is very difficult to define and measure the connection between violence and the media, experts such as Professor L. Rowell Huesmann of the University of Michigan argue that, "exposure to media violence causes children to behave more aggressively and affects them as adults years later."[105] Other research suggests that media violence has become much more graphic, sexual, and sadistic.

> *Explicit pictures of slow-motion bullets exploding from people's chests, and dead bodies surrounded by pools of blood, are now commonplace fare. Millions of viewers worldwide, many of them children, watch female World Wrestling Entertainment wrestlers try to tear out each other's hair and rip off each other's clothing. And one of the top-selling video games in the world,* Grand Theft Auto, *is programmed so players can beat prostitutes to death with baseball bats after having sex with them.*[106]

---

[104] See joint statement by the American Medical Association, the American Academy of Pediatrics, the American Psychological Association, and the American Academy of Child and Adolescent Psychiatry was released on July 26, 2001 at a public health summit in Washington D.C. "How media affects youth culture," www.negativemedia.htm. " A study completed by the Kaiser Family Foundation entitled "Kids & Media at The New Millennium" states that American youth spend 38 hours each week consuming media with "unsupervised television viewing" as the major media of choice." Study also suggests that ¾ of the public find television too violent. visited on February 28, 2003.

[105] See "Research on the Effect of Media Violence, Media Awareness Network," http://www.media-awareness.ca/english/issues/violence/effects_media_violence.cfm, visited on June 21, 2005.

[106] Ibid. See: "Violence in Media Entertainment," "Between 2000 B.C. and 44 A.D., the ancient Egyptians entertained themselves with plays re-enacting the murder of their god Osiris – and the spectacle, history tells us, led to a number of copycat

Whether or not we can agree with the aforementioned reports, the media and violence is a hot policy issue in America. On one hand, there is the 1st Amendment of the U.S. Constitution that ensures free speech and freedom of the press. On the other hand, there is a wide public outcry for the protection of children from unsuitable and violent media content.

Obviously, there are no simple solutions to this matter. American policymakers still face a great strain in the attempt to uncover a fair and satisfactory solution. The long-term solution should perhaps be focused on preventing the promotion of the culture of violence. Step one would logically entail educating the American people on the notion that aggression and violence are not the most just choices. Before this step can even be reached, however, the country must first come to admit the error of its ways – an error that was horrifically brought to light during the Columbine massacre. Shortly after the violence in Colorado had stopped, Bill Clinton suggested that, "We do know that we must do more to reach out to our children and teach them to express their anger and to resolve conflict with words, not weapons."[107]

The problem is not just with youth and the American school system, however. Many Americans are dissatisfied with the government, refusing to trust their elected officials. Representative Al Swift[108] summarized this claim when he said, "As a society, we don't trust anybody anymore. All the priests you don't know are hypocrites, all the teachers you don't know are incompetent, all the politicians you don't know are corrupt. There's a tremendous belief that none of our institutions are working."[109] Consequently, some citizen's work to form memberships with various movements founded upon the idea of distrusting the government. These groups predominantly ally themselves with the extremist right. These groups are, by nature, mainly racist and fascist and are composed of mostly white members. The Ku Klux Klan and the Neo-Nazis (best known as Arian Nations rooted in the Christian Identity Movement) are two examples of such

---

killings. The ancient Romans were given to lethal spectator sports as well, and in 380 B.C., Saint Augustine lamented that his society was addicted to gladiator games and "drunk with the fascination of bloodshed."

[107] See CNN Archives, "As Many as 25 Dead in Colorado School Attack," http://www.cnn.com/US/9904/20/school.shooting.08/, April 1999.

[108] Uslaner, Eric M. "The Decline of Comity in Congress," Chapter 4: "Values, Norms and Society," (Ann Arbor: The University of Michigan Press, 1993), Pg. 63.

[109] Ibid.

groups. These groups are small in number, but are among the most hateful extremist groups in America. Together – and trained with today's highly sophisticated weaponry – they represent a very real and serious danger.[110] Other dangerous groups include the "Patriots" – a highly political and well-armed paramilitary movement that believes a large and powerful American federal government and bureaucracy has too much control over its citizens. The "Patriots" tend to believe that federal regulations – such as paying taxes, gun control legislation, and regulation of farmers' land – are measures taken by the government to directly threaten civil liberties and independence.[111]

Several former associates of this group took action to destabilize the nation on April 19, 1995. U.S. citizens were stunned by this most horrifying domestic terrorist attack. The bombing of the Alfred P. Murrah Federal Building in Oklahoma City, Oklahoma, "killed 168 people, including 19 children in the America's Kids day-care center located on the structure's second floor. Approximately 600 persons were injured."[112] Perhaps the most humbling of facts surrounding the attack was that the perpetrators were American citizens, Timothy J. McVeigh and Terry Nichols. Although never a member, McVeigh was an outspoken and passionate promoter of the "Patriots" views in his antigovernment actions. He was tried and convicted of the bombing and was put to death by lethal injection on June 11, 2001.[113]

Today, Timothy McVeigh is a household name. His actions are regularly used to justify the existence and practice of the death penalty in America. He has become the proverbial poster boy for capital punishment – a cold-blooded mass-murderer whose name has joined the pantheons of notorious killers such as Adolph Hitler, John Wayne

---

[110] Abanes Richard: "American Militias, Rebelion, Rasizm and Religion," foreword by Roy Innis, Chairman, Congress of Racial Equality (C.O.R.E.), (Downers Grove, Illinois: Intervarsity Press 1996), Pg. 3-68. Also see: "Extremism in America: A Reader," edited by Lyman Tower Sargent, (New York and London, New York University Press, 1995), Pg. 9-10, 136-139, and 146.

[111] Abanes Richard: "American Militias, Rebelion, Rasizm and Religion," foreword by Roy Innis, Chairman, Congress of Racial Equality (C.O.R.E.) (Downers Grove, Illinois: Intervarsity Press 1996). Pg. 3- 68.

[112] Ibid. Also see Sarat Austin: "When the State Kills: Capital punishment and the American Condition, "Introduction: "If Timothy McVeigh Doesn't Deserve to Die, Who Does?" (Princeton and Oxford: Princeton University Press, 2001), Pg. 4-19.

[113] See: "American Terrorist, Timothy McVeigh & The Oklahoma City Bombing" by Lou Michel and Dan Herbeck, (New York, Regan Books, an Imprint of Harper Collins Publishers, 2001). See CNN Special Report, In –Depth Specials: http://www.cnn.com/SPECIALS/2001/okc/, March 7, 2003.

Gacy, and Jeffrey Dahmer.[114] One alternate, authentic, and thorough explanation of how a decorated war hero from rural New York State became the worst mass murderer in U.S. history (suggested in the book *American Terrorist*, by Lou Michel) leaves one with many questions about American society and their system of justice.[115]

As noted in the previous chapter, in many of the over 4,000 death row cases that lead to a conviction, the condemned did not have adequate defense lawyers or even proper trials. In addition, more than half of the condemned are nonwhites and indigent. Their cases receive little or no national publicity – unlike McVeigh, Dahmer, or Gacy; all middle-class white males. Many will argue that McVeigh's crime justifies the ultimate punishment but they cannot explain why American society breeds such hateful acts. Neither can they suggest that society has become less violent or safer after his death.

Why, then, does America still employ the death penalty? According to Zimring, what separates the U.S. from Western Europe is the profound difference in policy. In the United States, the death penalty is regarded as an issue of criminal justice policy – a matter for provincial governments to determine rather than a basic question for the central government. Another difference is the long-standing commitment in America to due process protections in criminal trials and opportunities for appellate review. By Yackle's analysis, however, the most important safeguard in the American criminal justice system against the possibility that innocent people may be executed (the *Writ of Habeas Corpus*) has been limited by the enactment of the Antiterrorism and Effective Death Penalty Act of 1996. This Act is so demanding that almost all prisoners that attempt to file federal appeal are destined to fail.[116] As Yackle concludes, "The Supreme Court and Congress have compromised the one procedural mechanism that might

---

[114] Sarat Austin: "When the State Kills: Capital Punishment and the American Condition," Introduction: "If Timothy McVeigh Doesn't Deserve to Die, Who Does?" (Princeton and Oxford: Princeton University Press, 2001) pg 11.

[115] See: "American Terrorist, Timothy McVeigh & The Oklahoma City Bombing" by Lou Michel and Dan Herbeck, (New York, Regan Books, an Imprint of Harper Collins Publishers, 2001).

[116] See Stephen P. Garvey, "Beyond Repair? America's Death Penalty," Postscript: "The Peculiar Present of American Capital Punishment," by Franklin E. Zimring, (Durham and London: Duke University Press, 2003), Pg 214-216. Also see: Leonard A Stevens, foreword by Michael Meltsner, Columbia University School of law, "Death Penalty, the Case of Life vs. Death in the United States, Great Constitutional Issues: the Eight Amendment," (New York: Coward, McCann & Georhean, Inc. 1978).

catch mistakes before it is too late: the federal court's authority to examine prisoners' constitutional claims in federal Habeas Corpus proceedings."[117]

Today, courts in the United States are prepared, by Sarat's account, to accept that some innocent people will be executed, as Justice Rehnquist observed in *Herrera v. Collins*: "due process does not require that every conceivable step be taken, at whatever cost to eliminate the possibility of convicting an innocent person."[118] Instead of a necessary safeguard, *Habeas Corpus* seems to be little more than a sacrifice of time and effort, serving no real purpose. The restrictions imposed upon federal *Habeas Corpus* proceedings are the subject of the next chapter.

---

[117] See Stephen P. Garvey, "Beyond Repair? America's Death Penalty," Chapter 2: "Capital Punishment, Federal Courts, and the Writ of Habeas Corpus," by Larry W. Yackle, Pg. 60. See also Antiterrorism and Effective Death Penalty Act www.berkeleycopwatch.org/cwreports/dec2001/antiterrorism.htm, visited on April10, 2003. "In response to the Oklahoma City bombing, President Clinton signed the Antiterrorism and Effective Death Penalty Act or ATA on April 24, 1996. This legislation did much to erode the Bill of Rights: It gutted the writ of habeas corpus, by eliminating federal constitutional review of state death penalty cases. It allowed the INS to deport immigrants based on secret evidence. It made it a crime to support the lawful activities of an organization labeled as a terrorist group by the State Department. It allowed the FBI to investigate the crime of material support for terrorism based solely on activities protected under the 1st Amendment. It froze assets of any US citizen or domestic organization believed to be an agent of a terrorist group, but it did not specify how an "agent" would be identified as such."

[118] See Sarat Austin: "When the state kills, Capital punishment and the American Condition," Chapter 9:Conclusion (Princeton, New Jersey: Princeton University Press, 2001), Pg 256.

Chapter Three

The Procedural Obstacles in the Path of the Last Hope

The restrictions upheld by the Supreme Court and Congress on federal Habeas Corpus in capital cases

The death penalty in the United States is a matter of state law and policy – this is to say that defendants are charged with state offenses and then tried, convicted, and sentenced in state courts. Defendants in capital cases are entitled to special procedural protections established by the 8th Amendment's prohibition on cruel and unusual punishment. In situations wherein any of the federal safeguards were being violated, defendants can press their federal claims on appeal to state appellate courts. After completion of the state appeal, the next phase is post-conviction proceedings in the state court in which the prisoner was convicted. These appeals are usually petitions or motions seeking an order of vacating the conviction or sentence based on new evidence that did not come at a trial or on appeal from the conviction.[119] Most capital prisoners also seek the U.S. Supreme Court review, which the

---

[119] See Stephen P. Garvey, "Beyond Repair? America's Death Penalty," Chapter 2: "Capital Punishment, Federal Courts, and the Writ of Habeas Corpus," by Larry W. Yackle, (Durham and London: Duke University Press, 2003), Pg. 61-62. Also see Michael Meltsner, "Cruel and Unusual, The Supreme Court and Capital Punishment," (New York: Random House, 1973).

Court occasionally grants, and that decision is viewed as a part of the state post-conviction inspection phase.[120]

Common knowledge is that the Supreme Court sets its agenda by choosing to hear certain cases and refusing to hear others. In other words, the Court selects cases that present questions of broad significance for society. *"In a real sense, then, the Court accepts cases not to correct lower courts' mistakes in those cases, but rather, to use the selected cases as vehicles for elaborating federal law for society at large."*[121]

As Dow noted, *Habeas* proceedings begin with the filing of a petition in a U.S. district court in the state in which the defendant was convicted. If the defendant's petition is denied, he/she may appeal to a federal circuit court and try to demonstrate that his/her petition presents substantial constitutional claim. In the event that the district court opinion is affirmed, the defendant may appeal to the Supreme Court. Despite the fact that that federal *Habeas Corpus* law is extremely complex, there is no constitutional right to have an attorney present during the process.[122]

Federal courts have had the authority to issue the *Writ of Habeas Corpus* since 1867. In the mid-twentieth century, the Supreme Court elaborated the writ's function with respect to state criminal convictions in a series of well-known opinions by Justices Holmes, Frankfurter, and Brennan. In the 1960s, *Habeas Corpus* provided that the lower federal courts enforce the Supreme Court's innovations in constitutional criminal procedure. In the 1970s and 1980s, the Supreme Court developed restrictive procedural doctrines to govern federal *Habeas*

---

[120] See Dow R. David and Mark Dow: "Machinery of Death, The Reality of America's Death Penalty Regime," with a foreword by Christopher Hichens, Chapter I: "How the Death Penalty Really Works," by David R. Row, (New York and London, Routledge, 2002), Pg. 14. "Technically, the inmate files a petition for a writ of certiorari; the Supreme Court, however, is not required to hear the merits of the case, and in fact very few death penalty cases are considered by the Supreme Court during the direct appeal phase."

[121] See Stephen P. Garvey, "Beyond Repair? America's Death Penalty," Chapter 2: "Capital Punishment, Federal Courts, and the Writ of Habeas Corpus," by Larry W. Yackle, (Durham and London: Duke University Press, 2003), Pg. 63.

[122] See Dow R. David and Mark Dow: "Machinery of Death: The Reality of America's Death Penalty Regime," with a foreword by Christopher Hichens, Chapter I: "How the Death Penalty Really Works," by David R. Row, (New York and London, Routledge, 2002), Pg.16- 19. Also see Appendix C in Appendices.

proceedings.[123] The Antiterrorism and Effective Death Penalty Act of 1996 – an Act that was approved by Congress and signed by then-President Bill Clinton, additionally limited the existing restrictions by the Court. Most provisions of this Act create procedural requirements that prisoners must satisfy before federal courts can consider their claim. Essentially, the purpose of these requirements is to streamline and expedite *Habeas Corpus* in federal court; but the new procedural demands are much more complicated and carry specific time limits within which appeals must be made. Prisoners in both capital and non-capital cases typically must file federal petitions within a year after the date on which the state court judgment in question becomes final. As for prisoners under sentence of death, they must file their claim within 180 days after their sentences are affirmed. Accordingly, filing periods do not expedite *Habeas Corpus* litigation, but often make it even more time-consuming. "Andrew Cantu was executed in 1999 after failing to obtain a further review of his case because he had not complied with this one-year deadline."[124]

Proponents of the death penalty insist that the establishment of the Antiterrorism Act was the right thing to do because, they say, prisoners under sentence of death are using *Habeas Corpus* only to extend

---

[123] See Michael Meltsner, "Cruel and Unusual, The Supreme Court and Capital Punishment," Chapter 2: "The Court," (New York: Random House, 1973). Pg. 20-45. Also see, Stephen P. Garvey, "Beyond Repair? America's Death Penalty," Chapter 2: "Capital Punishment, Federal Courts, and the Writ of Habeas Corpus," by Larry W. Yackle, (Durham and London: Duke University Press, 2003), Pg. 63. Rehnquist Court and Congress have assaulted federal habeas corpus on three general fronts. First, the court has limited the content of many of the constitutional rights that prisoners seek to vindicate in federal court and, in so doing, has sometimes largely excluded certain claims from the purview of federal habeas. Second, the Court and Congress have restricted federal court authority to address and vindicate constitutional claims that the state courts 'reasonably' have (or might have) rejected. Third, both the Court and Congress have erected procedural hurdles that petitioners must clear in order to press constitutional claims in federal court."

[124] See Dow R. David and Mark Dow: "Machinery of Death: The Reality of America's Death Penalty Regime," with a foreword by Christopher Hichens, Chapter I: "How the Death Penalty Really Works," by David R. Row, (New York and London, Routledge, 2002), Pg.16- 19. and Pg. 83-84. Also see: Roger Hood: "The Death Penalty: A World-Wide Perspective," 3d ed., Chapter 5: "Protecting the Innocent," Pg. 161. (New York, Oxford University Press, 2002). Also see Appendix C in Appendices.

litigation, thus, postponing lawful executions.[125] On the other side of the argument stands the American Bar Association – an organization that has always recognized the link between the death penalty and federal *Habeas Corpus* and, with little or no success, has opposed the enactment of this Act.[126]

In 2002, according to the Death Penalty Information Center, capital punishment has become more geographically isolated within the United States. Harries and Cheatwood have also concluded that:

> *Crime control, like crime itself, has distinctive regional flavors, with regional cultural values reflected quite effectively in the legislative process, as illustrated in struggles over handgun control in the U.S. Congress in 1988 and 1991. Capital punishment shares in this regional distinctiveness, states' rights having allowed the states to decide both whether they would have capital punishment at all and, if so, what methods would be used to carry it out.*[127]

From 1976 to the present, executions have occurred almost exclusively in the South – in particular, the state of Texas – accounting for three times the total of the West, Midwest and Northeast states combined (as this source reports and as Figure 1.3. illustrates). Figure 2.3 shows executions by region.[128] A wide range of economic and cultural reasons for the large concentration of capital punishment in southern states have been suggested.[129]

---

[125] Ibid. Pg. 59. Also see Charles L. Black Jr. "Capital Punishment: The Inevitability of Caprice and Mistake," 2d.ed., Chapter 8: "After Sentencing: Appeal, Post-Conviction Remedies, Clemency," (New York, London, Toronto: W.W. Norton & Company, 1981), Pg.79-84.

[126] See American Bar Association, Legislative and Governmental Advocacy, http://www.abanet.org/home.html, visited on April 10, 2003.

[127] Harries Keith and Derral Cheatwood, "The Geography of Executions, The Capital Punishment Quagmire in America," Chapter 4: "The Geography of Capital Punishment and Homicide: Regions of Violence," (Lanham, Boulder, New York, London: Rowman & Littlefield Publishers, Inc., 1997), pg.61.

[128] See Death Penalty Information Centre, http://deathpenaltyinfo.org/article.php?scid=8&did=146, visited on April 18, 2003. for Figure 1.3.and http://deathpenaltyinfo.org/article.php?scid=8&did=186, for Figure 2.3.

[129] Harries Keith and Derral Cheatwood, "The Geography of Executions, The Capital

Figure 1.3

Total since 1976 (including 2003): 846 Executions in 2003: 26

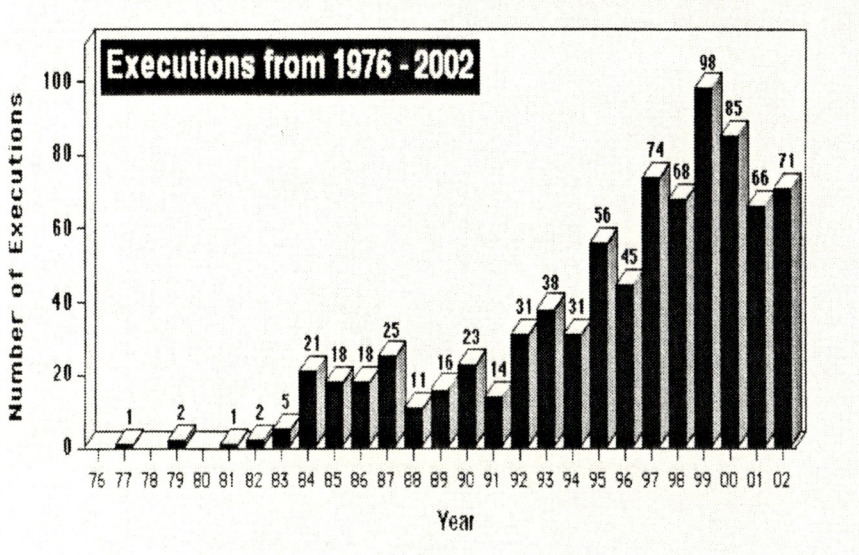

Source: Death Penalty Information Center, April 18, 2003.

Punishment Quagmire in America," Chapter 4: "The Historical Geography of Capital Punishment in America," (Lanham, Boulder, New York, London: Rowman & Littlefield Publishers, Inc., 1997), Pg. 30.

Figure 2. 3

EXECUTIONS BY REGION

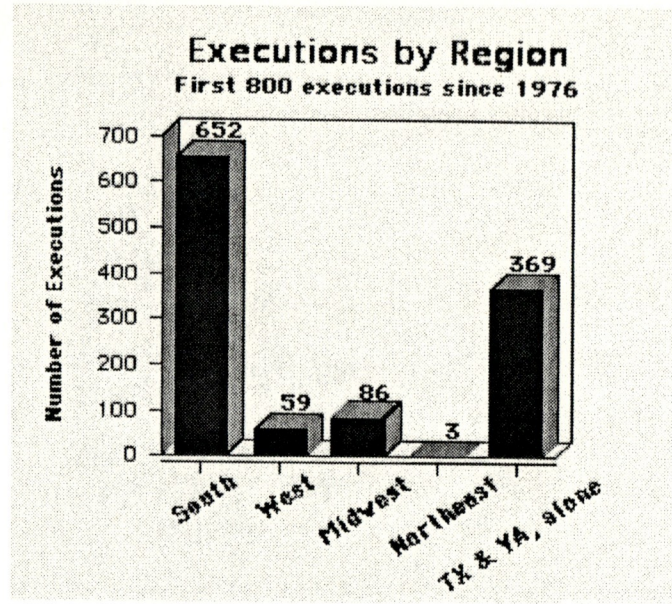

Executions By Region To Date
South 694
West 59
Midwest 90
Northeast 3
Texas and Virginia, alone 388

(Executions thru September 24, 2002)

Source: Death Penalty Information Center, April 12, 2003.

Noteworthy here is that, in 2002, the U.S. Supreme Court issued two landmark death penalty decisions. First, with *Atkins v. Virginia*, the Court ruled that the execution of inmates with mental disabilities is a violation of the constitutional ban on cruel and unusual punishment. Second, with *Ring v. Arizona*, it was determined that it is unconstitutional for a judge (rather than a jury) to decide on the presence of factors that make a case eligible for the death penalty. The latter ruling has sparked changes in many states. Florida and Alabama, however, maintain that judges can override jury recommendations in capital cases.[130]

In addition to these landmark rulings, two federal judges in unrelated cases held that the existing death penalty is unconstitutional. In New York, Judge Jed S. Rakoff found in *United States v. Quinones*

---

[130] See Death Penalty Information Centre, Year End Report, 2002, http://deathpenaltyinfo.org/yrendrpt02.pdf, visited on April 12, 2003.

that, according to recent revelations, it is likely that innocent people have been executed and that the current system was inadequate to prevent this deprivation of fundamental rights.[131] In *United States v. Fell*, Judge William Sessions in Vermont noted that, "Capital punishment is under siege." He called on Congress to decide if the death penalty is appropriate at all, saying, "If the death penalty is to be a part of our system of justice...standards and safeguards governing the kinds of evidence juries may consider must be rigorous and constitutional rights and liberties scrupulously practiced."[132]

These cases could very well mark a broad shift toward the abolition of capital punishment in America. If this is the case, an examination of the penalty that stands to replace it – a life sentence without the possibility of parole – is warranted. As Gallup reports, when given the sentencing alternative of life without the possibility of parole, 52% of Americans support the death penalty and 43% favor life imprisonment.[133]

A well-known opponent to the death penalty, Hugo Adam Bedau, favors long-term imprisonment. His detractors suggest that it is impossible to say which punishment is the more severe – but, according to Bedaue, one is, at the very least, clear:

> *Death is interminable, whereas it is always possible to revoke or interrupt a life sentence. Death also makes compensation impossible, whereas it is possible to compensate a prisoner in some way for wrongful confinement even if it is not possible to give back any of the liberty that was taken away. Death eliminates the presupposition of all experience and activity: life itself. For those reasons, the death penalty is unquestionably the more severe punishment, no matter what a few despondent life-term prisoners or sentimental observers my think they prefer, and no matter how painless and dignified the mode of execution might be.*[134]

---

[131] Ibid.
[132] Ibid.
[133] See the Gallup Poll Organization, Gallup News Service, May 20, 2002, visited on Feb.7, 2003.
[134] See Hugo Adam Bedau, "Death is Different: Studies in the Morality, Law, and Politics of Capital Punishment," Conclusion, (Boston: Northeastern University Press, 1987), Pg. 246.

American citizens tend to believe that a sentence to life imprisonment is more expensive than an execution. The reverse is true, in fact. Capital punishment trials are longer and incomparably more costly than keeping a criminal alive and productive in prison. According to the Death Penalty Information Center *"Florida spent an estimated $57 million on the death penalty from 1973 to 1988 to achieve 18 executions – that is an average of $3.2 million per execution."* The same source reports: *"In Texas, a death penalty case costs an average of $2.3 million, about three times the cost of imprisoning someone in a single cell at the highest security level for 40 years."*[135]

It has been stated that executions in the United States are the most humane because they are administered by professionally trained people. The frequency, however – to say nothing of the toll taken by carrying out the executions themselves – is extremely draining to the prison guards, wardens, executioners, and (most of all) the families of the victims and the condemned persons.[136]

An opinion by Shirley Carr – a parent that lost two sons in two separate shootings – reads as follows: "We don't pretend like this is behind us or put to rest but we deal with it by focusing on the positive things. And you can't do that if all your emotions are tied up with the D.A. and the system looking for revenge."[137] Revenge is certainly inherent to the concept of capital punishment – despite the efforts of the legal world to convince the public of the contrary. "Revenge," Shklar argues, "is an urge lurking in the shadows, whose presence provides reason for the founding of the modern state, and whose continuing force fuels the apparatus of punishment."[138] Hence, the sense of revenge present in the American system of justice serves as a reminder that, "modern legal orders are built on the edge of fear and anger, and that they must walk a fine line in their efforts to allay that fear and calm that anger."[139]

---

[135] See Death Penalty Information Centre, Cost of the Death Penalty, http://deathpenaltyinfo.org/article.php?did=108&scid=7#financial%20facts, visited on May 2, 2003.

[136] Dow R. David and Mark Dow: "Machinery of Death: The Reality of America's Death Penalty Regime," with a foreword by Christopher Hichens, Chapter 10: "The Stopping Point: Interview with a Tie-Down Officer," by Stacy Abramson and David Isay, (New York and London, Routledge, 2002), pg.169-173.

[137] See Michael Kroll, "Pro Life Parents," Mother Johns, Feb March 1990. Pg.13.

[138] See Sarat Austin: "When the state kills, Capital punishment and the American Condition," Chapter 2:"The return of revenge: Hearing the voice of the victim in capital trials," (Princeton, New Jersey: Princeton University Press, 2001), Pg. 43.

[139] Ibid. pg 58.

Conclusion

Since the reinstatement of capital punishment in 1976, public opinion on the death penalty has changed very little while support for death penalty reform and moratoriums on executions seems to have grown. The debate over capital punishment has shifted from a question of right or wrong to a question of whether the system can be "fixed". This shift finds its center at the increased application (and reliability) of forensic DNA testing in capital cases. Clear evidence of mitigating factors such as racism, inadequate legal representation, coerced confessions, mistaken eye-witnesses, jailhouse snitches, corrupt police officers, and cheating prosecutors, has lately begun to force American citizens to seriously reconsider the fairness of the American criminal justice system. In July of 2000, the Senate Judiciary Committee approved the Innocence Protection Act, improving death penalty counsel and providing universal access to DNA testing.[140]

The encouraging developments outlined above – to say nothing of the influence of the rest of the Western world – might suggest that the abolition of the death penalty in America is possible. On the other

---

[140] See "The Gallup Organization: In-depth Analyses, The Death Penalty, Support for the Death Penalty Over Time," August 2002, by Jeffrey M Jones, http://www.gallup.com, visited on Feb. 7, 2003. Also see Governor Ryan's speech on the blanket commutation of Illinois Death Row inmates, http://www.stopcapitalpunishment.org/ryans_speech.html, visited on Jan. 12/2003. Also see Stephen P. Garvey: "Beyond Repair? America's Death Penalty," Chapter Three, by Ken Armstrong & Steve Mills "Until I Can Be Sure: How the Threat of Executing the Innocent Has Transformed the Death Penalty Debate," (Durham and London, Duke University Press, 2003), Pg. 94-121. Also see Scheck, Barry, Peter Neufeld and Jim Dwyer, "Actual Innocence, When Justice Goes Wrong and How to Make it Right," Chapters: 3 to 10 (New York: A Signet Book, New American Library, 2000). And see: The Justice Project, Campaign for criminal justice reform, http://justice.policy.net, visited on May 2, 2003.

hand, as long as politicians can feel comfortable with promoting the death penalty as a quick solution to violent crime (read, "a headline-grabber during reelection periods"), capital punishment may enjoy a long and stable lifespan.[141]

The end of the death penalty regime, perhaps, can come only because of what Sarat calls a "new abolitionism" – or, simply put, the actions of ordinary people dedicated to the abolition of the most severe punishment known to man. In other words, political culture, rather then public opinion, determines the passage of death penalty legislation. If this mass awakening is ever to occur, American society, as Zimring and Hawkins noted long ago, "will be caching up with itself."[142]

Until further research on the effects of the death penalty in America is conducted, and until some of the major defects in the system are corrected, a moratorium on capital punishment would seem to be a wise decision. As the American Bar Association stated: "Efforts to forge fair capital punishment jurisprudence have failed. Today administration of the death penalty is a haphazard maze of unfair practices with no internal consistency."[143]

Anything concerning the death penalty, its purpose, its effect, its cost, its methods as Bedau pointed out, exists simply because of their proponents and a public that needs to believe in this punishment.[144] The fact is, as Lifton and Mitchell wrote, that:

Capital punishment is a form of killing. However quick and efficient, an execution is a violent act that turns human being into a corpse. Executions *make use of a technical apparatus constructed solely for the purpose of killing an immobilized person. Behind that apparatus, and inseparable from it, is a bureaucratic apparatus that*

---

[141] See Death Penalty Information Center, The future of the Death Penalty in the U.S. A Texas- Sized Crisis, by Richard C. Dieter, Executive Director, DPC. May 1994, visited on May 8, 2003.

[142] See Franklin E. Zimring and Gordon Hawkins, "Capital Punishment and the American Agenda," Chapter 8: "The Path to Abolition," (Cambridge, New York, New Rochelle, Melbourne, Sidney, Cambridge University Press, 1986), Pg. 165. "America has outgrown the death penalty, but it is reluctant to acknowledge that fact in the 1980s."

[143] See The American Bar Association, Legislative and Governmental Advocacy, http://www.abanet.org/home.html, visited on April 10, 2003. Also see, "Death Penalty Representation Project in 1986," http://www.abanet.org/deathpenalty/, visited on Feb.7, 2003.

[144] See Hugo Adam Bedau, "Death is Different: Studies in the Morality, Law, and Politics of Capital Punishment," Chapter One: "A Matter of life and Death," (Boston: Northeastern University Press, 1987), Pg. 37.

includes politicians and prosecutors, judges and juries, and wardens and prison guards, among others. The entire system, as we have seen, is geared to soften or eliminate the harsh truth of the killing. [145]

As noted throughout this study, the death penalty system is clearly broken beyond repair. In addition, American state killing is applied with systematic bias against minorities and poor people. As more and more countries abolish capital punishment, which is seen as a violation of human rights in almost all western industrial democracies, America is the only place where the death penalty has made a comeback. The persistent use of capital punishment in the United States leads to the view that America is " a pariah nation that violets the human rights of its own citizens."[146]

Perhaps the best summary of the strange acceptance of the death penalty in America was given by the Senator Russell Feingold in his speech on the Federal Death Abolition Act of 1999":

We are nation that prides itself on the fundamental principles of justice, liberty, equality and due process. We are a nation that scrutinizes the human rights records on other nations. We are one of the first nations to speak out against the torture and killings by foreign governments. It is time for us to look in the mirror. [147]

It is maybe a time for American nation to re-think its support to the death penalty, same as two former Supreme Court Justices, Harry Blacman and Lewis Powell have done.

---

[145] See Robert Jay Lifton and Greg Mitchell, "Who Owns Death? Capital Punishment, the American conscience, and the end of executions," Part IV: "The End Of Executions", New York: Perennial, An Imprint of Harper Collins Publishers, 2000). Pg. 231.

[146] See: Illinois Coalition Against The Death Penalty: "What's Wrong With The Death Penalty?",http://www.icadp.org/page17.html, visited on January9th, 2003.

[147] See Congressional Record, Proceedings and Debates of the 106th Congress, Second Session, Vol.146, Washington, Tuesday, November 16, 2000, Nos. 163, "The Federal Death Penalty Abolition Act of 1999," http://www.senate.gov/~feingold/speeches/senflor/abolitionspeech.html, visited on Feb.28, 2003.

Justice Harry Blackman penned the following eloquent dissent in 1994: "From this day forward, I no longer shall tinker with the machinery of death. For more that 20 years I have endeavored indeed, I have struggled along with a majority of this Court, to develop procedural and substantive rules that would lend more than the mere appearance of fairness to the death penalty endeavor. Rather than continue to coddle the Court's delusion that the desired level of fairness has been achieved and the need for regulation eviscerated, I feel morally and intellectually obligated simply to concede that the death penalty experiment has failed. It is virtually self-evident to me now that no combination of procedural rules or substantive regulations ever can save the death penalty from its inherent constitutional deficiencies. The basic question does the system accurately and consistently determine which defendants 'deserve' to die? cannot be answered affirmative... The problem is that the inevitability of factual, legal, and moral error gives us a system that we know must wrongly kill some defendants, a system that fails to deliver the fair, consistent, and reliable sentences of death required by the Constitution."[148]

The possibility for error in the American justice system is simply too great that should allow further use of the death penalty. Moreover, "surveys consistently show that - when offered the alternative of life without the possibility of parole for a minimum of 25 years, plus restitution for the victim's family - support for the death penalty drops below 50%".[149]

If capital punishment is about to vanish from the American criminal justice system, all that really needs is a little push.

---

[148] See Congressional Record, Proceedings and Debates of the 106th Congress, Second Session, Vol.146, Washington, Tuesday, November 16, 2000, Nos. 163, "The Federal Death Penalty Abolition Act of 1999," http://www.senate.gov/~feingold/speaches/senflor/abolitionspeech.html, visited on Feb.28, 2003. "Justice Lewis Powell also had a similar change of mind. Justice Powell dissented from the Furman decision in 1972, which struck down the death penalty as a form of cruel and unusual punishment."

[149] See: Floridians for Alternatives to the Death Penalty, Public Opinion, http://www.fadp.org/, visited on August 4th, 2005.

America's Controversies

Appendix A

Authorized Methods and number of Executions since 1976 in 38 states with the death penalty

Method	# of executions by method since 1976	# of states authorizing method	Jurisdictions that Authorize
Lethal Injection	683	37 states + U.S. Military and U.S. Government	Alabama, Arizona, Arkansas, California, Colorado, Connecticut, Delaware, Florida, Georgia, Idaho, Illinois, Indiana, Kansas, Kentucky, Louisiana, Maryland, Mississippi, Missouri, Montana, Nevada, New Hampshire, New Jersey, New Mexico, New York, North Carolina, Ohio, Oklahoma, Oregon, Pennsylvania, South Carolina, South Dakota, Tennessee, Texas, Utah, Virginia, Washington, Wyoming, U.S. Military U.S. Government
Electrocution	151	10 states (Nebraska is the only state that requires electrocution)	Alabama, Arkansas, Florida, [Illinois], Kentucky, Nebraska, [Oklahoma], South Carolina, Tennessee, Virginia
Gas Chamber	11	5 states (all have lethal injection as an alternative method)	Arizona, California, Maryland, Missouri, [Wyoming]
Hanging	3	3 states (all have lethal injection as an alternative method)	Delaware, New Hampshire, Washington
Firing Squad	2	3 states (all have lethal injection as an alternative method)	Idaho, [Oklahoma], Utah

States in [brackets] authorize the method only if a current method is found unconstitutional (see state description, below, for more information).

Source: Death Penalty Information Center, May 2, 2003.[150]

---

[150] See Death penalty Information Center, "State by state Death Penalty Information – States With the Death Penalty," http://deathpenaltyinfo.org, visited on May 2, 2003.

Appendix B

UM Researchers Question Lethal Injection as a Form of Capital Punishment

4/14/2005

A letter written by researchers at the University of Miami Leonard M. Miller School of Medicine and published in The Lancet raises serious questions about lethal injection as a form of capital punishment. The letter in the April 16th edition of the prestigious international journal describes compelling evidence of inadequate anesthesia during executions.

Lethal injection generally consists of the sequential administration of sodium thiopental for anesthesia, pancuronium bromide to induce paralysis, and finally potassium chloride to stop the heart and cause death. Without anesthesia, the condemned person would experience suffocation and excruciating pain without being able to move or communicate that fact.

"Unlike in medical applications, anesthesia in execution has not been subjected to clinical trials or government regulation, nor have the practitioners received even basic training to do this," says David A. Lubarsky, M.D., M.B.A., professor and chairman of the UM Department of Anesthesiology and one of the letter's authors. "This caused us to wonder whether anesthesia methodology in lethal injection might be inadequate."

The research team, which also included University of Miami faculty Teresa Zimmers, Ph.D., and Leonidas G. Koniaris, M.D., and Virginia attorney Jonathan Sheldon who specializes in the legal defense of the condemned, used a combination of state records obtained under the Freedom of Information Act, along with personal interviews and sworn testimony of corrections officials involved in executions in Virginia and Texas. They also obtained autopsy toxicology results from 49 executions in Arizona, Georgia, North Carolina and South Carolina.

"The practice of lethal injection for execution perverts the tools of medicine and the trust the public has in drugs and clinical protocols. Although executioners use an anesthetic, the current dosages and means of administration do not assure that inmates are senseless to pain, particularly because inmates are not monitored for level of consciousness or depth of anesthesia," said Leonidas G. Koniaris,

M.D., associate professor of clinical surgery, cell biology and anatomy, and lead author of the letter.

"We found that 43 of 49 executed inmates had post-mortem blood anesthesia levels below that required for surgery, while 21 of those inmates had levels that were consistent with awareness," said Teresa Zimmers, Ph.D., research assistant professor of surgery who analyzed the data for the research.

"This study provides strong evidence that anesthesia methodology in lethal injection is flawed and that some inmates likely experienced awareness and profound suffering during execution," said Jonathan Sheldon. "While some think that the condemned deserve to suffer, our society long ago rejected the unnecessary infliction of pain in execution because it is contrary to our 8th Amendment prohibition against cruel and unusual punishment."

The researchers point out that physicians are ethically prohibited from participating in an execution, so adequate anesthesia cannot be assured by physicians actively overseeing the process. For that reason, they believe that until better protocols are developed and tested and those delivering the executions are better trained to assure it is performed in a humane and competent fashion, execution by lethal injection should be stopped to prevent unnecessary cruelty and suffering.

Source: Miller School of Medicine, University of Miami http://www.med.miami.edu/news/view.asp?id=396, visited on May 26, 2005.

Appendix C

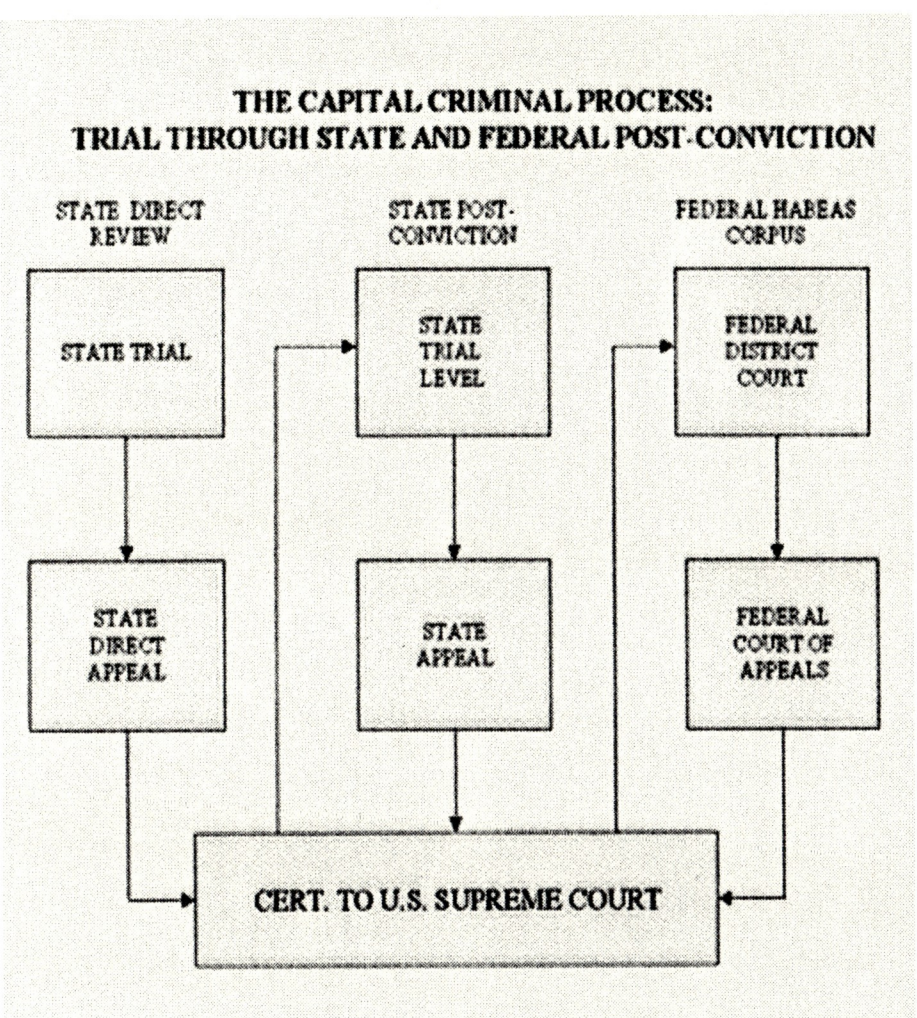

Source: The Justice Project, Campaign for Criminal Justice Reform, Liebman Study, The Capital Review Process, May 2, 2003.[151]

---

[151] See The Justice Project, Campaign for Criminal Justice Reform, Liebman Study, "A Broken System: Error Rates in Capital Cases, 1973-1995, The Capital Review Process," http://justice.policy.net/jpreport/section5.html#b, visited on May 2, 2003.

Bibliography

Abanes, Richard. 1996. "American Militias, Rebellion, Rasizm and Religion." Foreword by Roy Innis Chairman, Congress of Racial Equality (C.O.R.E.). Downers Grove, Illinois: Intervarsity Press.

Acker, R. James, Robert M. Bohm M. Robert, Charls S.Lanier, S.Charles.2nd.ed.2003. "America's Experiment with Capital Punishment", Carolina Academic Press, Durham, North Carolina

Amnesty International. 1979. "The Death Penalty." London: Amnesty International Publications.

_____ 1987. "United States of America: The Death Penalty." London, Amnesty International Publications.

_____ 1995. "The Machinery of Death: A Shocking Indictment of Capital Punishment in the United States. "New York: Amnesty International USA.

Baird, Robert M. and Stuart E. Rosenbaum 1995." Punishment and the Death Penalty, the Current Debate." New York: Prometheus Books.

Banner, Stuart. 2002. "The Death Penalty: An American History." Cambridge: Harvard University Press.

Bedau, Hugo Adam. ed. 1982. "The Death Penalty in America."3d ed. New York: Oxford University Press.

_____ 1987. "Death is Different: Studies in the Morality, Law and Politics of Capital Punishment." Boston: Northeastern University Press.

_____1984. "The Case Against the Death Penalty." New York: American Civil Liberties Union.

_____ 1988. "Capital Punishment." In Academic American Encyclopedia. Vol. 4, 123-124. Danbury, CT: Grolier.

_____ 1983. "Capital Punishment." In Encyclopedia of Crime and Justice. Vol.1, 133- 143, New York: Free Press.

_____ 1983. "Capital Punishment." In The Guide to American Law. Vol. 2.221-226. St. Louis, MO: West Publishing.

Bessler D. John. 1997. "Death in the Dark, Midnight Executions in America". Boston: Northeastern University Press.

Beth, Lren P. 1962. "Politics, the Constitution and the Supreme Court, An Introduction to the study of Constitutional Law". New York, Evanston, and London: Harper &Row Publishers.

Billings R. Paul. M.D. Ph.D. 1992. Vice Chairman, Department of Medicine Chief, Division of Genetic Medicine, California Pacific Medical Center: "DNA on Trial, Genetic Identification and Criminal Justice". (New York: Library of Congress Cataloging- in- Publication Data, Cold Spring Harbor Laboratory Press.

Black L. Charles, Jr.1981.2d.ed. "Capital Punishment: The Inevitability of Caprice and Mistake". New York, London, and Toronto: W.W. Norton & Company.

Bowers, William J., Glenn L. Pierce and John F. Mc Devitt. 1984. "Legal Homicide: Death as Punishment in America." 1864-1892. Boston: Northeastern University Press.

_____ 1974." "Executions in America." Lexington, MA: Lexington Books. Carrington, Frank G. 1978. "Neither Cruel Nor Unusual." New Rochelle. New York: Arlington House.

Burke, Terry. Gaudenz, Dolf. Alec J. Jeffreys. Roger Wolff. 1991. "DNA Fingerprinting: Approaches and Applications." Basel, Boston, and Berlin: Birkhauser Verlag.

Chandler B. David. 1976. "Capital Punishment in Canada, A Sociological Study of Repressive Law. The Carleton Library No.94. Published by McClelland and Stewart Limited in association with the Institute of Canadian Studies, Carleton University.

C.H.S. Jayewardene. University Ottawa. 1977."The Penalty of Death, The Canadian Experiment. Lexington Books. Massachusetts, Toronto: D.C. Heath and Company.

Davis, Michael. 1996."Justice in the Shadow of Death: Rethinking Capital and Lesser Punishments." Lanham, Maryland, USA. Rowman & Littlefield Publishers, Inc.

Dogan Mattei and Domenique Pelassy. 1990. "How to Compare Nations, Strategies in Comparative Politics", 2d.ed.Chatham, New Jersey: Chatham House Publishers, Inc.

Dow, David R. and Mark Dow. 2002. with Foreword by Christopher Hitchens. "Machinery of Death, the Reality of America's Death penalty Regime" New York and London: Routledge.

Farley, Mark A. 1991. "Forensic DNA Technology". Chelsea: Lewis Publishers, Inc.

Fry H. Earl. 1984. "Canadian Government and Politics in Comparative Perspective" Lanham, MD: University Press America.

Hood Roger. 2002."The Death Penalty, A world wide perspective", Third ed., New York: Oxford University Press.

Garvey P. Stephen. 2003. "Beyond Repair? America's Death Penalty". Durham and London: Duke University Press.

Gowers, Sir Ernest. 1956. "A Life for a Life? The Problem of Capital Punishment." London, Chatto and Windus.

Gray, Ian, and Moira Stanley, eds. 1989. "A Punishment in Search of a Crime: Americans Speak Out against the Death Penalty." New York: Avon Books.

Gross R. Samuel & Robert Mauro.1989. "Death & Discrimination, Racial disparities in Capital Sentencing. Boston: Northeastern University Press.

Hass, Kenneth C. and James A. Inciardi., 1988. "Challenging Capital Punishment, Legal and Social Science Approaches" Newbury Park: SAGE Publications, the Publishers of Professional Social Science.

Harries, Keith and Derral Cheatwood, *1997*. "The Geography of Executions, The Capital Punishment Quagmire in America". Lanham, Boulder, New York, London: Rowman & Littlefield Publishers, Inc.

Heineman, Robert A., Steven A. Peterson and Thomas H. Rasmussen, 1989"American Government". New York, Toronto: McGraw-Hill Book Company.

Hood, Roger. 1996. "The Death Penalty, A world wide perspective". 2d. revised and updated ed. Oxford: Clarendon Press.

King Rachel. 2003. "Don't Kill in Our Names", Families of Murder Victims Speak Out Against the Death Penalty", Introduction, (Rutgers University Press, New Brunswick, New Jersey and London.

Kirby, Lorne T. 1990. "DNA Fingerprinting". New York, London, Tokyo, Melbourne, Hong Kong: Stockton Press.

Krawczak M. and J. Schmidtke, 1994. "DNA Fingerprinting". Institute for Human genetic, Hanover: Bios Scientific Publishers.

Lifton Jay Robert and Greg Mitchell. 2002. "Who Owns Death? Capital Punishment, The American Conscience, and the end of Executions". New York: Perennial, An Imprint of Harper Collins Publishers.

Lipset Martin Seymour. 1990. "Continental Divide, The Values and institutions of the United States and Canada". New York: Routledge.

_____. 1997."American Exceptionalism, A Double–Edged Sword". New York&London, W.W. Northon &Company.

Masur, P.Luis. 1989. "Rites of Execution, Capital Punishment and the transformation of American culture, 1776-1865". New York, Oxford: Oxford University Press.

Mayhew, David R. 2000. "America's Congress, Actions in the Public Sphere, James Madison Through Newt Gingrich", New Haven and London: Yale University Press.

Michael Meltnsner. 1973. "Cruel and Unusual, The Supreme Court and Capital Punishment. New York: Random House.

Michel Lou and Dan Herbeck. 2001. "American Terrorist, Timothy McVeigh & The Oklahoma City Bombing". New York, Regan Books, an Imprint of Harper Collins Publishers.

McClellan, Grant S., ed. 1972. "Capital Punishment." Chicago: Aldine-Atherton.

McGuire, Kevin T. and Barbara Palmer, "Issues, Agendas, and Decision Making on the Supreme Court," The American Political Science Review, Vol. 90, No.4. (Dec.1996), Pg 853-865.

McGuire, Kevin T. "Amici Curiae and Strategies for Gaining Access to the Supreme Court", Political Research Quarterly, Vol. 47. Issue 4 (Dec.1994), Pg. 821- 837.

Miller, Arthur S., and Jeffrey Brown. 1988. "Death by Installments: the Ordeal of Willie Francis." Westport, CT: Greenwood Press.

Nelson Lane and Burk Foster. 2001. "Death Watch: A Death Penalty Anthology." New Jersey: Prentice Hall.

Pritchett, Charles, Herman. 1967."The American constitutional system", 2d.ed.New York: McGraw Hill.

Savoie, Donald J. 1999. "Governing from the Centre, The Concentration of Power in Canadian Politics". Toronto, Buffalo, London: University of Toronto Press.

Sarat Austin. 2001. "When the state kills, Capital punishment and the American Condition," Princeton and Oxford: Princeton University Press.

Sargent, Tower, Lyman. 1995. *"Extremism in America"*, A Reader, New York and London, New York University Press.

Schabas, William A. 1996. "The Death Penalty As Cruel Treatment and Torture, Capital Punishment Challenged in the World's Courts". Boston: Northeastern University Press.

Scheck Barry, Peter Neufeld and Jim Dwyer, 2000. "Actual Innocence, When Justice Goes wrong and how to make it right. New York: A Signet Book, New American Library.

Schwed, Rodger E. 1983. "Abolition and Capital Punishment: The United States Judicial, Political, and Moral Barometer." New York: AMS Press.

Shipman, Marlin. 2002. "The Penalty is Death, U.S. Newspaper Coverage of Women's Executions". Columbia and London: University of Missouri Press.

Stevens, Leonard A. 1978. Foreword by Michael Meltsner, Columbia University School of Law, "Death Penalty, the Case of Life vs. Death in the United States". New York: Coward, McCann & Geoghegan, Inc.

Stonecash, Jeffrey M., Mark d. Brewer & Mack D. Mariani.2003. "Diverging Parties, Social change, Realignment, and Party Polarization". Cambridge and Oxford, Westview Press.

Sundquist, Jams L. 1981."The Decline and Resurgence of Congress", Washington, D.C.: The Brookings Institution.

Tonry Michael and Richard S. Frase. 2001. "Sentencing and Sanctions in Western Countries," New York: Oxford University Press.

Uslaner, Eric M. 1993."The Decline of Comity in Congress". Ann Arbor: The University of Michigan Press.

Wilson Q. James, 1990."American Government, Brief Version". Lexington, Massachusetts, Toronto: D.C. Health and Company.

Woodward, Bob, and Scott Armstrong. 1979." The Brethren: Inside the Supreme Court. "New York: Simon and Schuster.

Zimmernman, Isidore. 1973. "Punishment Without Crime." New York: Manor Books

Zimring, Franklin E., and Gordon Hawkins. 1986. "Capital Punishment and the American Agenda." New York: Cambridge University Press.

Articles and Publications

"Death Penalty: cruel and even more unusual punishment." The Economist. No.303 (May 2, 1987): pg. 24-25.

Beltrame Julian: "Aimed at the heart, the U.S. capital trembled-then waved the flag", Canada's Weekly Newsmagazine Maclean's, "Special report after the terror,"September 24, 2001. Pg.40.

Fotheringham, Allan. "Between life and death row." Maclean's, No. 100 (April 13, 1987) Pg. 52.

Gelman, David. "The Bundy carnival: A thirst for revenge provokes a raucous stand-off." Newsweek, No. 113 (February 6, 1989) pg. 66.

Kaplan, David A. "Breaking the death barrier." Newsweek, No. 115 (February 19, 1990) Pg. 72-73.

_____ Death rides a judicial roller coaster: an inmate's fate." Newsweek No.115 (January 22, 1990) Pg.55.

Kroll, Michael. "Pro-life parents: Their children were murdered. Still, they oppose the death penalty." Mother Jones No 15 (February-March 1990) pg.13.

Press, Aric. "Gridlock on death row: the U.S. Supreme Court rejects a key challenge to capital punishment." Newsweek No. 109 (May 4, 1987) Pg 60.

Rosenbaum, Ron. "To young to die?" The New York Times Magazine No. 138 (March 12, 1989) Pg. 32-35.

Stout, David G. "The lawyers of death row: long hours and low pay in the battle against capital punishment." The New York Times Magazine No. 137 (February 14, 1988) Pg. 46.

"Innocence and the Death Penalty: the Increasing Danger of Executing the Innocent" (1997) Death Penalty Information Center, U.S.A.

"Millions Misspent: What Politicians Don't Say about the High Costs of the Death Penalty." (1994- Revised Edition) Death Penalty Information Center, U.S.A.

"Sentencing for Life: Americans Embrace Alternatives to the Death Penalty." (1993) Death Penalty Information Center, U.S.A.

"The Abolition of the Death Penalty in International Law." (1993 Cambridge, England: Gratis Publications.

Web Pages

The Innocence Project:
http://www.innocenceproject.org/about/index.php
Visited on Jan.10/2003.

ABC News, Opinions on Gun Issues,
http://abcnews.go.com/sections/us/DailyNews/guns_poll990518.html

ACLU on line archive:
http://www.aclu.org
Visited on Feb. 2, 2003.

The American Bar Association, Legislative and Governmental Advocacy:
http://www.abanet.org/home.html
Visited on April 10, 2003.

The American Bar Association, *"Death Penalty Representation Project in 1986"*:
http://www.abanet.org/deathpenalty/
Visited on Feb.7, 2003.

The American Medical Association, the American Academy of Pediatrics, the American Psychological Association, and the American Academy of Child and Adolescent Psychiatry that was released on July 26, 2001 at a public health summit in Washington D.C. "How media affects youth culture"
www.negativemedia.htm
Visited on February 28, 2003.

Antiterrorism and Effective Death Penalty Act:
http://www.berkeleycopwatch.org/cwreports/dec2001/antiterrorism.htm
Visited on April10, 2003.

The Canadian Government, "About Government, Political Parties:
http://canada.gc.ca/main_e.html
Visited on April 7, 2003.

CNN com, In –Depth Specials:
http://www.cnn.com/SPECIALS/2001/okc/,
Visited on March 7, 2003.

CNN Archive, Sniper Shootings:
http://wwwcgi.cnn.com/2002/LAW/11/04/sniper.shootings/
Visited on March 2003.

Congressional Record, Proceedings and Debates of the 106th Congress, Second Session, Vol.146, Washington, Tuesday, November 16, 2000, Nos. 163, "The Federal Death Penalty Abolition Act of 1999:
http://www.senate.gov/~feingold/speaches/senflor/abolitionspeech.html
Visited on Feb.28, 2003.

The U.S. Department of Justice, Office of Justice Programs, Bureau of Justice Statistic,
Special Report:
http://www.ojp.usdoj.gov/bjs/glance/exe.html.pdf
Visited on Feb. 4, 2003.

The U.S. Department of Justice, Office of Justice Programs, Bureau of Justice Statistics Publications:
http://www.ojp.usdoj.gov/bjs/pubalp2.htm,
Visited on April 8.2003.

Death penalty Information Center, State by state Death Penalty Information- States With the Death Penalty:
http://deathpenaltyinfo.org,
Visited on May 2, 2003.

Death Penalty Information Center, Year End Report, 2002:
http://deathpenaltyinfo.org/yrendrpt02.pdf
Visited on April 12, 2003.

Death Penalty Information Center, Cost of the Death Penalty:
http://deathpenaltyinfo.org/article.php?did=108&scid=7#financial%20facts
Visited on May 2, 2003.

Death Penalty Information Center, Countries that have been abolished the death penalty since 1976:
http://www.deathpenaltyinfo.org/article.php?scid=30&did=140#1976
Visited on April 8, 2003.

Death Penalty Information Center," The Death Penalty in Black and White: Who Lives, Who Dies, Who Decides" – "Executive Summary", by Richard C. Deither, Esq. Executive Director, Death Penalty Information Centre, June 1998:

http://www.deathpenaltyinfo.org/article.php?scid=45&did=539#Executive%20Summary, Visited on August 8,2005.

Governor Ryan's speech on the blanket commutation of Illinois Death Row inmates:
http://www.stopcapitalpunishment.org/ryans_speach.html
Visited on Jan. 12/2003.

The Gallup Organization, In-depth Analyses, The Death Penalty, support for the Death Penalty Over Time, August 2002, by Jeffrey M Jones:
http://www.gallup.com
Visited on Feb. 7, 2003.

The Gallup Poll Organization, Gallup News Service, May 20, 2002, Visited on Feb.7, 2003.

The Justice Project, Campaign for criminal justice reform
http://www.justice.policy.net/ipa/#4
Visited on Feb.4, 2003.

MSNBC NEWS:
http://www.msnbc.com/news/870343.asp?0cv=KB10
Archive June 3, 2000.
Visited on Jan.30, 2003.

Media Awareness Network, "Research on the Effects of Media Violence"
http://www.mediaawareness.ca/english/issues/violence/effects_media_violence.cfm Visited on June 21, 2005.

OYEZ, U.S. Supreme Court Multimedia, Roper v. Simmons, 543 U.S. ___ (2005) Docket Number: 03-633, Abstract:
http://www.oyez.org/oyez/resource/case/1724/
Visited on March 2, 2005.

Statistic Canada, "Justice and Crime, Homicide rate"
http://www.statcan.ca/english/Pgdb/legal01.htm
Visited on April 8, 2003.

Washington post, Nation, Gun Control:
http://www.washingtonpost.com/wpdyn/nation/specials/socialpolicy/guncontrol/
Visited on March 7, 2003.

Assessing the Legacy of Bill Clinton's Presidency

Will he be remembered for more than just the issues surrounding his impeachment?

By **Ksenija Arsic**
June 11, 2002

Introduction

On September 2, 1998, William Jefferson Clinton, the 42nd President of the United States, was first questioned by reporters about his sexual relationship with a former intern named Monica Lewinsky. In the months that followed, the American and world public learned the shameless details of President Clinton's adultery through accounts presented by the media. On December 19, 1999, over lies about sex, Clinton became the second President in American history to be impeached by the House of Representatives. On February 12, 1999, censure was proposed as the resolution and punishment for Clinton. "The United States Senate does hereby censure William Jefferson Clinton, President of the United States, and does condemn his wrongful conduct in the strongest terms."[152]

Public figures were, are, and always will be under the microscope. In order to be fully accountable to the citizens, they *should* be

---

[152] "The Breach, Inside the Impeachment and Trial of William Jefferson Clinton," The New York Times Bestseller, by Peter Baker, Appendix Four, Pg. 454, paperback edition, September 2001. Published by the Berkley Publishing Group, New York.

scrutinized. However, the question is how much detailed information about the sexual and personal life of a public figure has the public at large a right to know? Are these matters a fundamental issue for American politics and the American people? Does "freedom of the press" suggest the means to abuse a public figure or, in this case, can it be chalked up to a simple lack of taste?

Is American society all about personal destruction and modern-day crucifixion? Despite the many successes of the Clinton administration both domestically and internationally, it seems that the impeachment will forever overshadow its accomplishments. Among Clinton's historical achievements is the passage of the Family and Medical Leave Act, the lowest unemployment rate in 40 years, a strong economy, the establishment of the North American Free Trade Agreement (NAFTA), and the General Agreement on Tariffs and Trade (GATT) that ultimately lead to the World Trade Organization, permanent normalized trade relations with China, and the initiation of peace talks regarding Ireland and the Middle East.[153] Yet, the most prominent question remains: Was the American Presidency permanently damaged by President Clinton's adultery?

In order to answer this question, this essay will first attempt to explain the manner in which history has judged Presidents based on their accomplishments and achievements. The institution of the Presidency and the significance of the highest office in the United States of America will also be discussed. In addition, the impact of the impeachment, not only on the office of the President, but on Clinton himself and on the American society as a whole will be examined.

Overall, the Clinton Presidency promoted a number of successful domestic and foreign policies. The Lewinsky scandal shook the Presidency and threatened to have a long-lasting impact – but, essentially, it affected Clinton as an individual rather than the institution of the Presidency. Unfortunately, Clinton will always be remembered for the sex-scandal that led to his impeachment and not for his political successes. Many articles, analyses, and books were passionately written in order to explain Clinton and his era – yet largely failed to solve the puzzle about how such a charismatic and successful

---

[153] "The Postmodern Presidency, Bill Clinton's Legacy in U.S. Politics," by McCormick James M. Chapter 3: "Clinton and Foreign Policy, Some Legacies for a New Century," Pg 74-75. Edited by Shier Steven E. Pittsburgh, 2000/ University of Pittsburgh Press.

American leader could ruin his own public legacy by making such an extraordinarily poor decision on the intimate level.

According to Klein, maybe Clinton and his Presidency was misunderstood because he was governing during a time of peace and security in the late 20th century – at that point, people cared very little about politics and politicians. Clinton perhaps thought that he would get away with the Lewinsky affair because, in a time when the majority of Americans were leading comparatively fulfilling lives, people mostly wanted to be left alone, caring little about anything outside of their own agendas.[154] There was and is an alarming level of civic apathy in America.[155] Overall, participation and civic engagement has been declining in the U.S. for the last thirty years. Americans have become increasingly detached from their families, neighbors, communities, and society in general.

Moreover, after a series of deplorable political affairs – among them: the Vietnam War and Watergate – Americans started to distance themselves from the government and politics. Some general reasons for such civic withdrawal include the introduction of women into the workforce, major demographic shifts, a higher level of divorce, lower wages, pressures of time and money, generational differences, and new technology.[156] In addition, instead of the voluntarism so prevalent around the 70s and 80s, today's American society is shaped by powerful professional organizations specializing in fundraising and lobbying for political campaigns or interest groups.[157]

With these trends in mind, it is easy to suggest that maintaining dignity and a focused agenda within the office of the President has become a much more difficult task. Presidents like Bill Clinton have tried and (to a certain degree) have succeeded:

---

[154] "The Natural: The Misunderstood Presidency of Bill Clinton," by Joe Klein, Pg. 216-217, Published by Doubleday, division of Random House, Inc. April 2002, New York.

[155] "Bowling Alone: The Collapse and Revival of American Community," by Robert D. Putnam, Section I, Introduction, Chapter 1: "Thinking about Social Change in America," Pg. 19, and Section II: "Trends in Civic Engagement and Social Capital," Pg. 66-113, Published by Simon and Schuster, 2000, New York.

[156] Ibid. Section, III: "Why," Chapters: 10 to 14: Pg. 205 – 284.

[157] Ibid. Pg. 320-389,

Bill Clinton conducted a serious, substantive Presidency. His domestic policy achievements were not inconsiderable and were accomplished against great odds. He had rescued the Democratic Party from irrelevance and pursued a new philosophy of governance that made public-sector activism plausible once more, even in a time of national apathy and skepticism. Moreover, he performed the most important service that a leader can provide. He saw the world clearly and reacted prudently to the challenges he faced; he explained a complicated economic transformation to the American people and brought them to the edge of a new era...He may be remembered as the President who served before history resumed its contentious dance, before life got serious again.[158]

---

[158] "The Natural: The Misunderstood Presidency of Bill Clinton," by Joe Klein, Pg. 216-217, Published by Doubleday, division of Random House, Inc. April 2002, New York.

Evaluating the Presidents of the United States of America

From the time of the writing of the American Constitution to the present, the Presidency and performances of the Presidents have been the central issues of interest and analysis for political scientists, sociologists, psychologists, the media, and American civil society. A wealth of theories, studies, articles and books have been written in attempt to explain and define the most important part of the American political system: the Executive Office of the Presidency.

Rating the Presidents became a matter of professional interest in 1948 when Arthur M. Schlesinger, a history professor at Harvard University, collected the views of 55 historians and published them as a poll in *Life Magazine*. 14 years later, another poll was taken and published in the *New York Times*.[159] Although the public embraced Schlesinger's polls, many historians criticized them because the samples lacked the opinions of women, minorities, or even southerners. The most prominent historian to have criticized this poll, Professor Thomas A. Bailey, said that attempting to rank the Presidents is equivalent to "measur[ing] the immeasurable." [160] Despite early difficulties to create a perfect and universal formula for evaluation of the Presidency, new attempts were forged in subsequent years – each adding details regarding contemporary values and overall changes within society.[161]

Because the Presidency is both an institution and an individual, it has proven very difficult to establish a universal formula for all times and all circumstances.

---

[159] "Greatness in the White House, Rating the Presidents, Washington through Carter," Final Report, The Presidential Performance Study, by Robert K. Murray and Tim H. Blessing/ 1988, The Pennsylvania State University, Pg. 1-6.
[160] Ibid. Pg. 7.
[161] Ibid. Pg. 10.

In 1982, a new survey, called the *Murray-Blessing Ratings*, was initiated. This poll called for 1,997 questionnaires to be sent to all Ph.D.-carrying American historians listed in the American Historical Association's Guide to Departments of History for 1979-1980 and 1980-1981.[162] The survey consisted of 180 questions and was followed up by face-to-face interviews. In many ways, it has contributed to a better understanding of the human factor that influences Presidential ratings. The poll rightly took into consideration the fact that Presidents are elected during certain times, under certain conditions, and with an inherited agenda and problem set. This being the case, personal abilities such as intelligence, political prowess, problem solving skills, and desire to make a difference were the most significant factors used to determine Presidential rankings. The four-part survey questioned participants about presidential leadership in a number of areas and concluded by asking participants to rank presidents in one of six categories: Great, Near Great, Above Average, Average, Below Average, and Failure. Almost half of the historians completed the questionnaire, and the results of the rankings showed few differences among the top-ranked presidents, with Lincoln, Washington, and Franklin D.Roosevelt again being the top three. This survey strongly indicated that future results would not substantially change existing rankings of the Presidents. *The Murray-Blessing Ratings* survey was invaluable in terms of improving the approach, methods, knowledge and technique regarding the ranking of the Presidents.[163]

Today, most Americans place their confidences in a poll established by and named for George Gallup. Most Gallup interviews are conducted by telephone from Gallup's regional interviewing centers around the country. Trained interviewers and today's (CATI) technology (assisted telephone interviewing that brings the survey questions up on a computer monitor) makes it possible for the results to be available immediately upon completion of the last interview.[164] In 2000, the Gallup Poll asked people to select the best and worst presidents. The results were as follows: "the seven highest-ranking presidents are: Kennedy, Lincoln, FDR, Reagan, Washington, Clinton, and George Bush, while the bottom five were Nixon, Clinton, Carter,

---

[162] Ibid. Pg. 10-22.
[163] Ibid. Pg. 22-24.
[164] See: The Gallup Poll Organization, "How are polls conducted?" by Frank Newport, Lydia Saad, David Moore from Where America Stands, 1997, John Wiley & Sons, Inc.http://www.gallup.com/help/FAQs/poll1.asp, visited on August 4, 2005.

Reagan and Bush. Of the twelve names at either end of this survey, six served in the past forty years, and three of those six were listed at both ends. Furthermore, while the top three presidents in all of the "expert" surveys were included in the top seven, Kennedy outranked all three, and Reagan outranked Washington. ". [165]

In October 2000, Hofstra University sponsored a symposium on "The Leadership Difference Rating the Presidents" to examine presidential ratings from a scholarly perspective. According to Bose's report on this Conference, comparing public and scholarly opinion on presidential ratings is useful because it can illustrate differences in criteria among respondents, which in turn may indicate different priorities. The substantial diffence, as Bose wrote, is that a popular Gallup survey typically is conducted over the telephone, and respondents are giving their immediate reactions. Scholarly surveys, in contrast, typically are conducted through the mail, which gives respondents time to evaluate their rankings. Furthermore, distance from a presidency, can serve to shape and even revise scholarly and popular assessments.[166]

On the other hand, as Bose noted, "C-SPAN's survey was especially interesting because it polled both scholarly and popular rankings, with consistent results at the top and bottom of each survey but some important differences in between. For example, Reagan ranked sixth in the viewer survey but eleventh in the historian survey."[167]

The symposium on presidential ratings its purposes, criteria, and consequences concluded that:

> *Presidential ratings surveys ultimately are useful because of the debates they provoke about individual presidents. In examining why certain presidents rank as Near Great in some surveys and Below Average in others, we learn about the*

---

[165] See: The Gallup Poll Organization: "Regan, Kennedy and Lincoln Receive the most votes for " Greatest U.S. President", by Wendy W. Simmons, http://www.gallup.com/poll/content/?ci=1984&pg=1' visited on August 4th, 2005.

[166] See: "Presidential ratings: lessons and liabilities" White House Studies, by Meena Bose, Wntr.2003, http://www.findarticles.com/p/articles/mi_m0KVD/is_1_3/ai_109025095, visited on August 4,2005.

[167] Ibid.

priorities of reviewers as well as differing interpretations of a president's accomplishments, shortcomings, and legacy. The greatest disagreement arises with twentieth-century presidents, particularly those who served in the past forty years, but these disputes are unsurprising. Future surveys would benefit from adopting some of the recommendations presented in the symposium, such as canvassing a wider range of reviewers, especially more experts on the nineteenth-century presidents.[168]

Each President throughout history was unique – some of them displaying extraordinary personalities and accomplishing significant things. These men shaped and changed the high opinion of the institution of the Presidency. Others were almost instantly forgotten after their term in office.

Bill Clinton was the first elected President in America to be impeached – excluding President Nixon who had resigned before the actual process began and President Andrew Johnson in 1868, who attained Office in the White House after the assassination of President Abraham Lincoln.[169]

---

[168] Ibid.

[169] See: "Rating the Presidents, A Ranking of U.S. Leaders, From Great and Honorable to the Dishonest and Incompetent," by William Ridings, Jr. and Stuart B. McIver, Pg.275. Published 1997, revised & updated 2000,KensingtonPublishingCorporation, New York. See also: "Main article: Impeachment in the United States ",
http://en.wikipedia.org/wiki/Richard_Nixon, visited on August 4, 2005.
" President Nixon was never impeached- he became the only president to resign from office under the threat of an inevitable impeachment." ..."Richard Nixon resigned after impeachment hearings against him started, though the House then voted without debate by 412-3 to "accept" the articles of Impeachment passed by the Judiciary Committee." Ibid. http://en.wikipedia.org/wiki/Andrew_Johnson, visited on August 4, 2005.
"The drive to impeach Johnson, the only President to be impeached and tried in the Senate, was really about the politics of post – Civil War Reconstruction. The Radical Republicans who controlled Congress took a hard line toward Dixie. Johnson was no Confederate. He was the only Southern Congressman not to secede when the state did. But he vetoed bills that he viewed as too punitive against former slave owners, and he resisted military rule over the Southern states. Technically, Johnson was impeached for firing his Secretary of War, Edwin Stanton, who was a Radical Republican sympathizer. Johnson's enemies said the dismissal violated the Tenure of Office Act, a law that was letter judged to be unconstitutional. The legislators threw in a few other charges, including conspiracy and bringing Congress into disrepute. "On Monday, February 24, at

Presidents come to office with a policy agenda that they try to fulfill during their term. In order for a President to be successful in achieving his goals, he must have public support – or, in other words, high approval rating.

> *The Presidency as an institution means whatever the President, Congress, the courts, the media, and the American people at any given point in history agree that it means. The process of arriving at that agreement – which is never complete and is always a matter of debate – is a complex series of negotiations which involve legislation, judicial decisions, media frames, and public opinion.*[170]

President Clinton and his administration depended heavily on polls. At first, polls were perhaps a positive – as they made the Presidency more accessible and popular and (to a certain degree) even demystified the job. But the high degree of intimacy with the public – instituted by the media of the times – had its own risks (as illustrated by the Lewinsky affair). Americans at large were perhaps attracted to the drama in the White House because it seemed to be such a close-knit part of their everyday lives. Most did not approve of the way the media handled the situation – as innuendo was passed off as news and unreliable leaks were presented as truth – yet, they could not resist absorbing the details. During the Clinton scandal, media ratings soared – resulting in the daily broadcast of the real-life soap opera for almost a full year.

The fact remains that public interest in the Presidency will always be very high but the question is, for what reason? Is it possible to clearly distinguish public news from private news, political from personal? Public figures will always be held under the proverbial microscope, will forever be forced to sacrifice the right to privacy granted to ordinary citizens. The President is perhaps the most susceptible because Americans tend to view him as the highest national

---

five o'clock p.m., when a vote was taken, and the resolution (which reads thus: "Resolved, That Andrew Johnson, President of the United States, be impeached of high crimes and misdemeanors") was adopted by a vote of 126 yeas to 47 nays."

[170] "Sex, Lies and Presidential Leadership: Interpretations of the Office," Presidential Studies Quarterly, vol. 30, no 3.3, September 2000, Pg. 514, by Mary E. Stuckey and Shannon Wabshall.

figure, rather like a father figure that protects and guides them. In this way, the President shapes the national identity; he dreams for the people; he is their role model.[171] The very nature of his position requires him to make face and give his all; be not unlike a god-man at all times.

Taking this into consideration, it can be suggested that Bill Clinton lost the moral authority of his office when the country learned of his indiscretions. It should be noted here that, even before Clinton, infidelity in the White House was a common issue of public knowledge. There was never quite the same frenzy surrounding these affairs, however. Joe Lieberman, the Democratic senator from Connecticut. explained that, in the media-drenched times that we live in, the President's private life had become public. He expressed deep concern over Clinton's act. Lieberman also suggested that such behavior was not just inappropriate and immoral, but very damaging, as well – as it tends to project a message to American families (in particular, America's youth) about what is and is not considered acceptable behavior.[172]

In addition to the moral critique by his Democratic comrades, President Clinton was bad-mouthed on a daily basis by many of his political opponents – most notably by the Independent Counsel, Kenneth Starr. Nevertheless, the question of whether or not Clinton's actions had risen to the level of "high Crimes and Misdemeanors" was never fully answered. In fact, it is perhaps true that Clinton's misdemeanor never completely fit with the constitutional standard for impeachment. According to Article II of the Constitution, only one sentence can be applied to the particular word 'impeachment' without specific definition, further guidance or even clear position on what is the meaning of "high Crimes and Misdemeanors". A more detailed definition of 'high crimes and misdemeanors' reads as follows:

> *High crimes and misdemeanors is a phrase from the United States Constitution,Article II, Section 4: "The President, Vice President and all civil officers of the United States, shall be removed from office on impeachment for, and*

---

[171] Ibid.
[172] "The Breach, Inside the impeachment and trial of William Jefferson Clinton," The New York Times Bestseller, by Peter Baker, Chapter One: " I don't know how we can get through this," Pg. 60, Paperback edition/ September 2001. Published by the Berkley Publishing Group, New York.

conviction of, treason bribery, or other high crimes and misdemeanors.

"High" in the legal parlance of the 18th century means "against the State". A high crime is one which seeks the overthrow of the country, which gives aid or comfort to its enemies, or which injures the country to the profit of an individual or group.

In democracies and similar societies it also includes crimes which attempt to alter the outcome of elections."[173]

The central and dividing issue during the impeachment of President Clinton was about the question did Clinton's perjury rose to the level of "high Crimes and Misdemeanors".

Despite the lack of a clear-cut definition for "high Crimes and Misdemeanors," Republicans in the House believed that Clinton's actions warranted impeachment. They failed to persuade the majority of Senators to agree, however. Democrats insisted that Independent Prosecutor Kenneth Starr was engaged in a zealous witch-hunt.[174] Along with Starr, many politicians and other public figures out to defame President Clinton admitted that the nature of the act that led to the scandal was not, in itself, an impeachable offense – but it did, in fact, lead to the crimes of perjury and obstruction of justice. The President, they said, had knowingly and repeatedly broken the law and had therefore violated his oath of office.[175]

Worldwide debate ensued. Does a sex cover-up fall under "high Crimes and Misdemeanors"? Lying about sexual conduct, at the very least, was enough to cause a constitutional crisis.

"Clearly, the Independent Counsel statute needs major changes. If an independent counsel like Starr cannot complete initial assignments (Travelgate and Filegate), the attorney general should not add other duties (Monica Lewinsky). Also, Starr pursued too many side activities: private litigation,

---

[173] See High Crimes and Misdemeanors, Wikipedia, The Free Encyclopedia http://en.wikipedia.org/wiki/High_Crimes_and_Misdemeanors, visited on August 4, 2005.

[174] "The Clinton scandal and the Future of American Government," edited by Mark J. Rozell and Clyde Wilcox, Introduction, Pg. 7– 22, Edition 2000. Published by the Georgetown University Press, Washington, D.C.

[175] Ibid. Pg. 7-22.

teaching, and speeches to organizations hostile to President Clinton. Independent counsels need to complete their work expeditiously and professionally."[176]

This is not to say that President Clinton should not have been investigated – no one, after all, is above the law. The argument here is the lack of balance in Starr's report. Starr knew that lying about sex was not the stuff of impeachment but he had been granted an unlimited budget and almost unlimited power to question everyone associated with Clinton and do whatever else was necessary (in his judgment) to expose the President and, ideally, remove him from the White House.[177] Though the move was unsuccessful, permanent damage was surely done. The American people will remember Clinton as the President who made a terrible mistake, darkening his legacy forever. On a more important note, "if an elected President could be removed by his political enemies on the basis of private misdoings and an effort to cover them up, the Madisonian system itself could be in danger of collapse."[178]

While judging the Presidents, it is essential to separate the institution from the person. Hence, the President's personality is the most relevant point when considering the accomplishments that shape his legacy. This is perhaps because the high moral standards and impeccable personal characteristics – by which such a significant portion of American government has been shaped – should always be a norm. The Presidency cannot be understood without consideration of the values that each President brings to the White House. The President represents and implements the American value system during his term. Judging such subjective points is no easy task – hence, the search for universal standards is a process constantly in flux, with a finish line that is perhaps impossible to reach. Just like Clinton himself, the Clinton Presidency was convoluted and complicated – it simultaneously represented the good and the bad. Given the contemporary social climate, it is likely that the 42nd President will be remembered for his

---

[176] "The Clinton scandal and the Future of American Government," edited by Mark J. Rozell and Clyde Wilcox, Introduction, Pg. vii-viii, Edition 2000. Published by the Georgetown University Press, Washington, D.C.
[177] Ibid. Pg. 1-15.
[178] "The American President," edited by Philip B. Kunhardt, Jr., Philip B. Kunhardt III, and Peter W. Kunhardt, "William Jefferson Clinton, 1993-2001," Pg. 434, Published by The Berkley Publishing Group, Riverhead Books, 1999, New York, NY.

character (and, more importantly, his weaknesses) rather than his substantial achievements that will be discussed in the next section of this paper.

The Clinton Presidency Before the Impeachment

The social polarization over Clinton's legacy clearly mirrors American political division along Party lines of the Democrats and Republicans. What will be written about his Presidency in the history books will depend very much upon who is doing the writing. One thing is for certain: nobody wanted to be President of the United States of America more than William Jefferson Clinton.

> *When he was sixteen years old, he went to Washington for the first time as a delegate to Boy's Nation and arranged to be in the best position in the Rose Garden to shake John Kennedy's hand. He came home not only with a picture of that iconic hand-shake, the symbolic transfer of power and ambition from one generation to the next, but also with a burning desire to someday be there to shake the hands of another generation of young men of Boy's Nation.*[179]

Taking the above into consideration, it is very difficult to understand why Clinton would jeopardize his life dream by engaging in a sexual affair with a young intern. According to many, the answer lies in his controversial personality. He is well known as a survivor with a seductive style, brilliant and capable of dealing with all kinds of policy issues. He always attended events, kept numerous appointments, and left almost no time for rest. Such behavior, as Stanley A. Renshon, a psychoanalyst and political scientist, argued in his book *High Hopes*

---

[179] "Power of the Presidency," by David McCullough, Chapter One, "What's Essential is Invisible," Pg. 137, edited by Robert A. Wilson, Published in 1999 by Public Affairs, New York.

could perhaps be explained by Clinton's desire to be constantly stimulated. "Clinton's behavioral pattern suggests that he frantically pursues not just work activity, but activity itself."[180] As Renshon noted, his fear of being alone and dealing with his own feelings originate from experiences that he had growing up in a troubled home. Whatever the reason, Clinton has always displayed a constant need to be liked. Perhaps this explains his obsession with opinion polls. He sincerely wanted to be praised and remembered as a great President. He worked hard to earn an honored place in American history – but he failed because of his "skirt problem".[181]

Even before his Presidency began, Bill Clinton was forced to defend his intimate life. Gennifer Flowers alleged to have carried on a twelve-year affair with Clinton. The information was issued on the cover of *Star Magazine* on the eve of the '92 Presidential election. In response, Clinton submitted to a joint interview with his wife, Hillary, in a famous interview on CBS' *60 Minutes*.

> *I have acknowledged wrongdoing. I have acknowledged causing pain in my marriage. I have said things to you tonight that no American politician ever has. I think most Americans who are watching this tonight; they'll know what we're saying. They'll get it, and they'll feel we've been more than candid.*[182]

Clinton's Presidency started with a clear lack of the high moral standards required for the office and faded away in the same manner.

The legacy of any President is dictated by the times. World War I characterized Woodrow Wilson's Presidency. The Great Depression and World War II dominated the Presidency of Franklin Roosevelt. During Harry Truman's term, there was the Korean War. For Lyndon Johnson, it was Vietnam.[183]

---

[180] "High Hopes, The Clinton Presidency and the Politics of Ambition" by Stanley A.Renshon, Pg. 58-59, Published 1996 by New York University Press, New York and London.

[181] "The Hunting of the President, The Ten-Year Campaign to Destroy Bill and Hillary Clinton," by Joe Conason & Gene Lyons, Chapter One: "The Ghost of Lee Atwater," Pg. 3, Copyright 2000, Thomas Dunne Books, An imprint of St. Martin's Press, New York.

[182] Ibid. Pg. 24.

[183] "Rating the Presidents, A Ranking of U.S. Leaders, From Great and Honorable to the Dishonest and Incompetent," by William Ridings, Jr. and Stuart B. McIver,

The air campaign over Bosnia and Kosovo aside, Bill Clinton's Presidency was one of peace and prosperity. Clinton inherited the biggest federal budget deficit in American history and still managed to reduce it. In fact, Clinton's Presidency saw the largest budget surplus ($69.2 billion for FY 1998 and $79.3 billion for FY 1999),[184] the lowest unemployment rate in more than 40 years, the fastest growth in real wages for more than two decades, and a significant drop in the number of people on the welfare.

His biggest failures included the ambitious health plan that originally was masterminded by the First Lady. Hillary Clinton had found success in piloting a similar effort toward school reform in Arkansas.[185] Healthcare, however, was a significant issue that almost every President had attempted to reform – and proved to be a much more daunting task. The Democrats and the Republicans both wanted reform but failed to reach an agreement on how to implement it. This inaction left an indelible mark on the Clinton Presidency – he was branded as a man who made many promises but delivered on few.

No one seemed to consider that healthcare reform efforts in the past had also failed miserably. Nor did the public care that the issues were terribly complex and opposing forces were well-financed. Clinton failed to live up to expectations, however lofty those expectations may have been. In the process, Clinton was accused of selling out, of compromising to the point where reform was meaningless.[186]

A combination of poorly presented issues and badly designed policy processes were to blame. His "universal coverage" that would provide "security and freedom," leading to a "choice" of doctors and

---

Pg. 174-252. Published 1997, revised & updated 2000,Kensington Publishing Corporation, New York.

[184] "Rating the Presidents, A Ranking of U.S. Leaders, From Great and Honorable to the Dishonest and Incompetent," by William Ridings, Jr. and Stuart B. McIver, Pg. 57 Published 1997, revised & updated 2000,Kensington Publishing Corporation, New York.

[185] "The Clinton Presidency, images, Issues, and Communication Strategies," by Rita K. Whillock, Chapter 6: "The Compromising Clinton: Images of Failure, A Record of Success" Pg. 133, Edited by Robert E. Denton, Jr. and Rachel L. Holloway, Published 1996, by Praeger Series in Political Communication Westport, Connecticut London.

[186] Ibid. Pg. 133.

healthcare plans sounded almost possible – but Clinton's call for "simplicity" belied the sheer size and complexity of the plan. Some 15.5% of the population still lacks basic health insurance. More than 10 million of these people are children.[187] As Holloway points out, two factors contributed directly to the President's inability to manage his involvement on this important issue. The first was Hillary Clinton's refusal to step aside and let someone else to try to finish the job. The second was the so-called "closed process" – a term that here refers to the complete exclusion of Republicans in consultations about the policy. In the end, said Holloway, the failure to pass healthcare reform led to a lack of confidence in the Clinton White House and greatly hindered the ability of a Democratic Congress to come up with a solution. This failure was reflected in the Congressional elections of 1994 – which saw the Republicans regain control over the House.[188]

During Clinton's long and unsuccessful battle over healthcare reform, personal conflicts were waged – including the Whitewater investigation and Paula Jones' sexual harassment suit. There were also significant international issues that needed to be addressed. Problems in Bosnia, Iraq, Rwanda and North Korea demanded the President's increasingly divided attention.[189] In respect to foreign policy, Clinton's main priority was a peace deal in the Middle East – but he fell short of that goal. His efforts in Northern Ireland were successful, however, resulting in resolving the conflict in Northern Ireland. As mentioned, President Clinton helped to negotiate the North American Free Trade Agreement (NAFTA) with Canada and Mexico despite substantial opposition from members of his own Party. According to Sharon D. Wright, NAFTA resulted in a loss of jobs in some trade-related industries near the U.S-Mexican border, leaving the impression that Latinos did not benefit from this agreement as they had hoped.[190] Noteworthy here, however, is Clinton's handling of race relations,

---

[187] Ibid. 134
[188] Ibid. Chapter 8: " The Clintons and the Health Care Crisis: Opportunity Lost, Promise Unfulfilled," by Rachel L. Holloway, Pg. 161-183.
[189] "The Clinton Presidency, Images, Issues, and Communication Strategies," by Rachel L. Holloway, Chapter 8: " The Clintons and the Health Care Crisis: Opportunity Lost, Promise Unfulfilled," Pg. 174, Edited by Robert E. Denton, Jr. and Rachel L. Holloway, Published 1996, by Praeger Series in Political Communication, Westport Connecticut London
[190] "The Postmodern Presidency, Bill Clinton's Legacy in U.S. Politics," by Sharon D.Wright, Chapter 11: "Clinton and Racial Politics," Pg. 230. Edited by Shier Steven E. Pittsburgh: 2000,University of Pittsburgh Press.

education, environment, crime and gender (all fields that were highly rated by the public) inherent in the implementation of NAFTA.[191] Clinton was arguably the first President in decades to put the interests of minorities on the national agenda. His was a significant positive impact on racial politics in America. Indeed, African Americans were very pleased with the President's attempt to include them in his government.

Counted among his successes is Clinton's crime bill – an action that provided funding for more police officers and more prisons, banned assault weapons, and placed tighter control on the purchase of handguns.[192] The Clinton administration also had a long-term impact regarding gender politics.

> *The Clinton Presidency has made women more visible in political leadership positions, most notably by appointing the first female Secretary of State and the first female Attorney General...The first piece of legislation President Clinton signed into law was the Family and Medical Leave Act, which enables workers to take up to 12 weeks of unpaid leave to care for a new baby or ailing family member without jeopardizing their job.[193]*

By Pitney Jr.'s account, President Clinton frustrated Republicans in the same way that President Nixon had done with the Democrats in the 1970s.

> *Both Nixon and Clinton enraged their political opponents by simultaneously demonizing them and poaching on their issues. Both raised concerns in Congress about usurpation of power. Nixon waged secret military operations and impounded funds, while Clinton bypassed Congressional authority through far-reaching executive orders. And, in both cases, the resulting anger and distrust created the climate for impeachment.[194]*

The overarching American sentiment was one of empathy. People simply felt that they knew President Clinton – that he understood and

---

[191] Ibid. Pg. 134.
[192] Ibid. Pg. 237.
[193] Ibid. Chapter 12:Pg. 239.
[194] " The Postmodern Presidency, Bill Clinton's Legacy in U.S. Politics," by John J. Pitney Jr., Chapter 8: "Clinton and the Republican Party," Pg. 177, Edited by Shier E. Steven, Pittsburgh: 2000, University of Pittsburgh Press.

realized their pain. They adored him for it. His job-approval ratings remained high even throughout the Lewinsky scandal. The public never displayed a sense of urgency when it came to the impeachment trial – and this was perhaps owed to their intense bond with the human side of their President. Low marks were given regarding his character, but high marks were given regarding his leadership.

Overall, before the Lewinsky scandal, Clinton's Presidency was regarded as a successful one. It is also perhaps fair to say that Clinton's Presidency was an important one. According to historians, in assessing the impact of the Clinton scandal on the Presidency, it is clear that the institution has been deeply wounded and is likely to be weakened in the future. Presidential scholar Thomas Cronin provides a dissenting opinion, however, and suggests that the institution of the Presidency will survive and it will not be too much affected by the Cliton scandal.[195]

It seems impossible to find a middle position regarding the rating of Clinton's terms in office. Whatever the truth may be, damage to the American Presidency has certainly been done. Some observers believe that the office was seriously damaged and abused long ago – during the Nixon Watergate scandal. Just as Nixon's indiscretion represented an abuse of executive privilege, so too did Clinton's.[196] According to Spitzer, however, despite the misuse of executive privilege, "no searching reassessment of the scope and consequences of Presidential power and authority occurred during or immediately after the Clinton impeachment effort, aside from analysis of the independent counsel law, the Jones case, and the like."[197] Public opinion has played an important role in this matter. Though the vast majority of Americans believed Clinton's actions to be morally reprehensible, their view of the Presidency remained relatively unchanged. People's disappointment, bitterness, and cynicism toward the government only deepened, supporting Putnam's theory of civic disconnection.

As far as public perception of future political scandals is concerned, "until they come to believe that leaders can offer both

---

[195] "The Clinton scandal and the Future of American Government," by Robert J Spitzer: "The Presidency: The Clinton Crisis and its consequences," Pg. 15, edited by Mark J. Rozell and Clyde Wilcox / 2000. Published by the Georgetown University Press, Washington, D.C.

[196] The Clinton scandal and the Future of American Government," by Robert J Spitzer: "The Presidency: The Clinton Crisis and its consequences," Pg. xvi. edited by Mark J. Rozell and Clyde Wilcox / 2000. Published by the Georgetown University Press, Washington, D.C.

[197] Ibid. Pg. 15.

personal virtue and successful governing or realize that private behavior affects public performance, it is likely that future Presidential scandals will be regarded by the public as business as usual."[198]

---

[198] "The Postmodern Presidency, Bill Clinton's Legacy in U.S. Politics," by Diane Hollern Harvey, Chapter 6: "The Public view of Clinton" Pg. 142, Edited by Shier Steven E. Pittsburgh, 2000 / University of Pittsburgh Press.

Clinton's Legacy After Leaving Office

Immediately upon finishing his term, a variety of rumors again brought unwanted attention to President and Hillary Clinton. This time, according to the press, the Clinton pair was questioned about the gifts and furniture they took when they left Washington. In addition, serious questions were raised about the pardons Clinton had issued on his last day in office. The most outrageous was the pardon to Marc Rich.

> *Before Clinton freed him from prosecution on his final full day in the White House, Rich was one of the Justice Department's most wanted international fugitives. The House Government Reform Committee opened its investigation into whether the eleventh-hour decision was linked to the more than $1 million Rich's ex-wife, Denise Rich, donated to Democratic causes, including then-first lady Hillary Rodham Clinton's Senate campaign.*[199]

The media even reported a farfetched possibility that Clinton's political enemies would try to impeach President Clinton again. It appeared that the constant controversy that surrounded Clinton's Presidency would never end – and that the media and his political opponents would not allow him to escape the spotlight.

After his Presidency, the Ridings McIver Presidential Poll stated that President Clinton was, "ranked twenty third of forty-one chief

---

[199] "Politics, power and money: The pardons controversy," article " Pardons may tarnish Clinton legacy Carol Clark, CNN writer/editor, from www.CNN.com/2001/Clinton/

executives, close to the center and positioned in the middle third of American Presidents."[200] Participants in this poll have indicated that somewhere between 25 and 50 years need to pass before a valid, rational evaluation of modern Presidents can be made. That interval, they say, "permits the emotions of the day to recede and it also permits future observers to perceive the true impact of any given administration's policies. Did they work, or not?"[201]

Almost all attempts to assess Clinton's legacy are largely based on the Lewinsky scandal. President Clinton, as Senator Bob Graham (D-FL) said: "dishonored himself and the highest office in our American democracy."[202]

---

[200] "Rating the Presidents, A Ranking of U.S. Leaders, From Great and Honorable to the Dishonest and Incompetent," by William Ridings, Jr. and Stuart B. McIver, Pg. 282. Published 1997, revised & updated 2000, Kensington Publishing Corporation, New York.

[201] Ibid. Pg. 283.

[202] "Rating the Presidents, A Ranking of U.S. Leaders, From Great and Honorable to the Dishonest and Incompetent," by William Ridings, Jr. and Stuart B. McIver, Pg. 275. Published 1997, revised & updated 2000, Kensington Publishing Corporation, New York.

Conclusion

Recently, Monica Lewinsky appeared on CNN's *Larry King Live*.[203] In a very active and candid interview, she discussed the fact that she enjoys talking to young audiences about her personal experience in the White House. Apparently, she is qualified enough to comment on constitutional- and law-related questions regarding privacy issues. Perhaps this *is* the case. After all, her name will be written in history books alongside President Clinton's – simply because she had the mind to keep a filthy dress that carried the President's DNA. Linda Tripp has undergone plastic surgery, hoping that the new look could save her from the criminal preceding that she is facing in Maryland for taping conversations she had with Lewinski.[204] Although Tripp maintains that, during the Clinton vs. Lewinsky matter, she was only doing the right thing. For many Americans, her name will forever be synonymous with spite, betrayal, and disgust. How depressing to think that the 42nd President will always be associated with the aforementioned names.

As Derrshowittz wrote:

> *If there was indeed a 'right –wing conspiracy' out there waiting to 'get' the President, it is difficult to imagine any action more reckless than the Oval Office sex with a young blabbermouth whose goal was probably as much to brag about her conquest of the President as to engage in an intimate relationship."* [205]

---

[203] CNN show "Larry King live" on February 26, 2002, interview with Monica Lewinsky.

[204] "Larry King, with Pat Piper, Anything Goes! What I've Learned from Pundits, Politicians, and Presidents," by Larry King, Chapter 8: "Whatever," Pg. 215-227, Published, 2000 by Warner Books Inc. New York.

[205] "Sexual McCarthyism, Clinton, Starr, and the Emerging Constitutional Crisis," by Alan M. Dershowitz, "How Did We Get Here?" Pg.7. Published 1998, by Basic Books, A Member of the Persues Books Group. New York, NY.

On the other hand, by Derrshovittz's account:

> *If it is true that consensual activity- an affair followed by an attempt to cover it up – is not the sort of 'high' crime contemplated as impeachable by our Constitution, than it is gratuitous, unfair and degrading to conduct extensive hearings into whether President Clinton did or did not touch specified portions of Monica Lewinsky's anatomy.*[206]

Clinton's eight years in the White House were filled with successes and failures, triumphs and defeats. He had this to say about the Presidency:

> *I think that the Presidency can still be a place of great influence and power; it's still the central office of the country, particularly in times of adversity or crisis. It can be in good times as well, but it requires a greater level of energy to advance. In other words, there's not an automatic deference to the Presidency. There's lot of checks, and not just in Congress, and not just when Congress is of the opposite party – although that certainly complicates things – but in the proliferation of press sources, in the fact that we no longer have as big a percentage of the world's wealth [as] we did in the end of the Cold War. All these things mean the energy level of the President, and the degree to which the President has thought about what the real challenges facing the country are, and specifically what the President should do about them, is more important than ever before. The President can still be very, very effective, but it requires more discipline and more care and a real plan to do that. But I still think it's the greatest job in the world and I still think it's very, very important to the American people.*[207]

Bill Clinton, like probably any other President upon finishing his term in the White House, only now knows how to be a President.

---

[206] Ibid. Pg.238.

[207] "The American President," edited by Philip B. Kunhardt, Jr., Philip B. Kunhardt III, and Peter W. Kunhardt, "William Jefferson Clinton, 1993-2001," Pg. 437. Published by The Berkley Publishing Group, Riverhead Books, 1999, New York, NY.

America's Controversies

After September 11, 2001, life got deadly serious in America and around the world. The response to this unexpected crisis from American citizens was an awakened patriotism and support to fight back. And America did just that. Only – after more than four years – it seems that the government did not meet all of the objectives that were set at the beginning of the Global War on Terrorism. And the future remains uncertain. People seem to be longing more and more for the "good old days" of the Clinton Presidency – despite the sex-scandal that led to his impeachment. In retrospect, it is easier to respect Bill Clinton as a man who was simply human. After all, "sex is politic and politic is sex, and never the twain shell be parted".[208]

---

[208] "Sexual McCarthyism, Clinton, Starr, and the Emerging Constitutional Crisis," by Alan M. Dershowitz, Chapter IV: "Monica Lewinsky: Is it about Sex or about lying about sex?", Pg.210. Published 1998 by Basic Books, A Member of the Persues Books Group. New York, NY.

Bibliography

Baker, Peter. "The Breach: Inside the Impeachment and the Trial of William Jefferson Clinton." September, 2001. Berkley Publishing Group. New York.

Clark, Carol. "Politics, Power and Money: The Pardons Controversy." CNN writer article, "Pardons May Tarnish Clinton Legacy." www.CNN.com/2001/Clinton.

Cohen, Jeffrey. "The Polls: Public Favorability toward the First Lady." 1993-1999. *Presidential Studies Quarterly*. September 1, 2000.

Conason, Joe & Lyons, Gene. "The Hunting of the President: The Ten Year Campaign to Destroy Bill and Hillary Clinton." 2000. Thomas Dunne Books. New York.

Denton, Robert E. Jr. & Holloway, Rachel L. "The Clinton Presidency: Images Issues and Communication Strategies." 1996. Praeger Series in Political Communication. Westport, Connecticut.

Dershowitz, Alan M. "Sexual McCarthyism: Clinton, Starr, and the Emerging Constitutional Crisis." 1998. Basic Books (A Member of the Perseus Books Group). New York.

Drew, Elizabeth. "Whatever It Takes." Updated edition, 1998. Penguin Books. New York, New York.

King, Larry with Piper, Pat. "Anything Goes! What I've Learned from Pundits Politicians and Presidents." 2000. Warner Books Inc. New York.

King, Larry. CNN show: *Larry King Live*. February 26, 2002. Interview with Monica Lewinsky.

Klein, Joe. "Eight Years: Bill Clinton and the Politics of Persistence." *The New Yorker*. October 16&23, 2000.

Klein, Joe. "The Natural: the Misunderstood Presidency of Bill Clinton." April 2002. Doubleday, a Division of Random House Inc. New York.

Kunhardt, Philip B. Jr. & Kunhardt, Philip B. III. "The American President: William Jefferson Clinton." 1999. The Berkley Publishing Group, Riverhead Books. New York, NY.

McCullough, David. "Power of the Presidency." 1999. Public Affairs. New York

McIver, Stuart B. & Ridings, William Jr. "Rating the Presidents: a Ranking of U.S. Leaders, From the Great and Honorable to the Dishonest and Incompetent." 1997. Revised & updated 2000. Kensington Publishing Corporation. New York.

Murray, Robert K. & Blessing, Tim H. "Greatness in the White House: Rating Presidents Washington through Carter." Final Report, *the Presidential Performance Study*. 1988. The Pennsylvania State University Press.

Putnam, Robert D. "Bowling Alone: The Collapse and Revival of American Community." 2000. Simon & Schuster. New York

Renshon, Stanley A. "High Hopes: The Clinton Presidency and the Politics of Ambition." 1996. New York University Press. New York and London.

Rozell, Mark J. & Wilcox, Clyde. "The Clinton Scandal and the Future of American Government." 2000. Georgetown University Press. Washington, D.C.

Shier, Steven E. "The Postmodern Presidency: Bill Clinton's Legacy in U. S. Politics." 2000. University of Pittsburgh Press. Pittsburgh.

Stephanopoulos, George. "All too Human: A Political Education." 1999. Little, Brown and Company. Boston, New York, and London.

Stuckey, Mary E. & Wabshall, Shannon. "Sex, Lies and Presidential Leadership: Interpretations of the Office." *Presidential Studies Quarterly*, Vol.30, no.3. September 2000.

The Official Report of the Independent Counsel's Investigation of the President. "The Starr Report." Forum (An Imprint of Prima Publishing). Rocklin, CA.

Web Pages:

The Gallup Poll Organization, "How are polls conducted?" by Frank Newport, Lydia Saad, David Moore from Where America Stands, 1997, John Wiley & Sons, Inc.
http://www.gallup.com/help/FAQs/poll1.asp,
Visited on August 4, 2005.

The Gallup Poll Organization:" Regan, Kennedy and Lincoln Receive the most votes for " Greatest U.S. President", by Wendy W. Simmons,
http://www.gallup.com/poll/content/?ci=1984&pg=1,
Visited on August 4th, 2005.

Presidential ratings: lessons and liabilities, White House Studies, by Meena Bose, Wntr.2003,
http://www.findarticles.com/p/articles/mi_m0KVD/is_1_3/ai_109025095, Visited on August 4,2005.

Wikipedia, The Free Encyclopedia, High Crimes and Misdemeanors
http://en.wikipedia.org/wiki/High_Crimes_and_Misdemeanors,
Visited on August 4, 2005.

Wikipedia, The Free Encyclopedia,
"Main article: Impeachment in the United States ",
http://en.wikipedia.org/wiki/Richard_Nixon, Visited on August 4, 2005.

Wikipedia, The Free Encyclopedia,
"Main article: Impeachment in the United States ",
http://en.wikipedia.org/wiki/Andrew_Johnson, Visited on August 4, 2005.

The American Dream

I have a dream that one day this nation will rise up and leave out the true meaning of its creed – we hold these truths to be self evident that all men are created equal...My country 'tis of thee, sweet land of liberty, of thee I sing. Land where my fathers died, land of the Pilgrim's pride, from every mountainside, let freedom ring! And if America is to be a great nation, this must become true. (The autobiography of Martin Luther King, Jr. by Clayborne Carson, 226-227)

Over thirty years ago, Martin Luther King, Jr. spoke about a dream that he had envisioned – the traditional "American Dream". His famous speech focused upon racism in America and the importance of equality. His far-reaching plan, the "Poor People's Campaign" (Carson, 226), and demand for full employment and the opportunity to secure jobs for all underprivileged Americans of all classes and races is still far from being fulfilled. Despite the fact that contemporary society still faces similar, if not the same, obstacles (socioeconomic inequality and racism), the magic of the American Dream is still alive, though perhaps somewhat changed. Nevertheless, after centuries of torment and struggle, can this dream be considered myth or reality? How many actually achieve it?

The American Dream is freedom, opportunity, justice, success, and equality (amongst other things). It is unique to one land but perhaps not attainable for all. For many, the American Dream is little more than a nightmare. Many authors have attempted to analyze the concept. Writers such as Jeffery Simpson and Robert Putnam believe that the American Dream, as an institution, is in dispute. The following pages will discuss how, in Simpson's *Star-Spangled Canadians* and in Putnam's *Bowling Alone*, these authors have approached the issue. The core message of these two works seems to be that of the American Dream as a much more complex engine than the average citizen realizes.

According to Simpson, like many immigrants motivated by the promise of a better life, Canadians are generally unwilling to openly admit the search for the American Dream – but emigrate to their southern neighbor for the same reason as any other: opportunity. Opportunity to earn more income; opportunity to more freely pursue their goals; opportunity to provide more financial security for their families; opportunity to test themselves in a bigger market and against tougher competition; opportunity to work with more resources and clusters of highly trained people; opportunity to work at the "cutting edge" – whether it be filmmaking, conducting research, driving innovation, negotiating deals, or practicing art. For them, America represents the opportunity to play on a bigger stage, before larger audiences, under brighter lights. (Simpson, 156)

America is a country of equal opportunity – but those who want to succeed must fight for their goals. An individual's ability and strength directly dictate his/her chances at success in this most Darwinist concept of the life game.

Many Star-Spangled Canadians quickly realize that the American Dream has another side of the coin. Poverty, crime, and racial conflict is commonplace in the U.S. Accordingly, many incline to think that violence is embedded in the American consciousness. A valid perception, considering its prevalence on film, television, radio, and in the most popular video games. Without explicitly denying this assumption, Simpson tries to explain that violence is depicted as mainly concentrated in the areas that are populated by African Americans that are poor. (Simpson, 82)

Putnam dissents. He believes that violence in America is spreading beyond the inner cities. "Social capital contributes to safe and productive neighborhoods, while its absence hampers efforts at improvement...The shooting sprees that affected schools in suburban and rural communities as the twentieth century ended are a reminder that as the breakdown of community continues in more privileged settings, affluence and education are insufficient to prevent collective tragedy." (Putnam, 318.)

In *Bowling Alone*, Putnam refers to social capital as social organizations such as networks, norms, and social trusts that facilitate coordination and cooperation for mutual benefit. (Putnam, 66) Life tends to be easier in a community with strong social capital. With it comes societal trust, better communication, and true civic involvement in all that is essential for the functioning of American democracy.

Overall civic engagement was very high in the early 1960s – as evidenced by the substantially larger voter turnout. Due to a variety of scandals (Vietnam, Watergate, etc.), Americans began to distance themselves from the government and politics – to say nothing of organizational memberships, religious participation, and volunteerism. Putnam's great allegory (hence, the title of his book), points out that, despite the sharp rise in the popularity of bowling, there are fewer organized leagues than ever before. To Putnam, the American desire to bowl alone, "illustrate[s] yet another vanishing form of social capital." (Putnam, 113)

As Putnam recognizes, there are a few key factors contributing to the erosion of social capital. Women have left the home and taken paying jobs, moving is more frequent, there are more divorces and fewer marriages, fewer children, (comparatively) lower wages, pressures of time and money, more solitary use of leisure time, new technology, etc. (Putnam, 205-284) The voluntarism that was so prevalent around the 70s and 80s has been replaced by professional organizations specializing in lobbying and fundraising for political campaigns or interest groups. These groups have become powerful political forces that shape American society. New mass-membership organizations such as the Sierra Club or even "Red Sox Nation" are, in a sense, politically important but their ties in terms of social capital do not exist. (Putnam 380 – 389)

In the last chapter of his book, Putnam provides some hints as to how to change the actual approach to the problem by identifying efforts that can be forged by the individual.

"My intention in this chapter is the modest – to identify key facets of the challenge ahead by sketching briefly six spheres that deserve special attention from aspiring social capitalists: youth and schools, the workplace, urban and metropolitan design, religion, arts and culture, and politics and government."(Putnam, 404) Essentially, Putnam's strong belief in reviving the American civic engagement is the key answer for improving all of the aforementioned six spheres.

Serious decline in civic engagement in America, however, appears to suggest that the search for new organizations and networks that could generate more social capital will take a while. At the same time, the eventual awakening and remobilization of the growing numbers of Americans that question the effectiveness of their established government and other sociopolitical institutions will not be without intrigue.

In addition, the concept of a politicized civil society is a precondition for other countries that are going through the democratization process. How will they achieve high civic engagement, then, while well-established democracies are already experiencing the same problem? With all of the aforementioned dilemmas and questions in mind, it may prove to be difficult to keep the magic of the American Dream alive.

Finally, many believe that the events of September 11, 2001 have led to a new way of life and politics in America as well as the world at large and have changed inevitably ideal of the American Dream The ensuing American global war against terrorism has led to new domestic security measures at American airports, border crossings, and other sensitive locations. Simple acts such as going to the store, attending a concert or sporting event, or catching a movie are routinely interrupted by security guards inspecting bags and using hand scanners to check for metal weapons or explosives. On the international scale, Americans have learned that there are rebel groups and even entire nations fanatically dedicated to the destruction of the North American way of life, that is, the American Dream. The national consciousness has come to realize that it can no longer afford to ignore the rest of the globe. (MacLean's Newsmagazine, report by Allan R. Gregg Pg. 34, October 15/2001) This is the new American reality, not a dream of equality and freedom.

American Foreign Policy towards Cuba

Self-portrayed as "exceptional and generally superior to most other" nations, American foreign policy follows loose tenants of progress. The overarching themes are those of ending hunger, disease, and poverty, and promoting democracy around the world. Despite this focus, the U.S. failed to accomplish any of these tenants with one of its closest neighbors, Cuba. (International human rights, by Jack Donnelly, Pg. 87) Incoherent U.S. policy toward Cuba only deepened the existing gap. Despite wide belief that a change in U.S-Cuban policy is unlikely as long as Fidel Castro remains in power, lately, the government has displayed signs of a shift toward improvement and reform. The dialogue between these two countries has gone from self-serving to mutually beneficial over the course of the past few years.

The first portion of this chapter will focus on American-Cuban policy from the Bay of Pigs to the Helms Burton Act and how this policy was counterproductive to American interests. The second part of the chapter will discuss the lessons that could be derived from this experience – and perhaps applied to the shaping of future American foreign policy toward Cuba.

The Cuban Revolution challenged U.S. might and debunked the myth of U.S. domination over Latin America. Determined to circumvent the spread of communism – especially in a country so close to home – the U.S. made the move to quash the Cuban Revolution. The Bay of Pigs invasion backfired when Castro's forces intercepted the 1400 Cuban exiles organized by the Central Intelligence Agency as they landed. This defeat seriously weakened the anti-Castro movement, response, and the United States. In the latter country imposed an economic embargo banning all trade with and travel to its southern neighbor. (Dunning 214-215.)

In 1962, John F. Kennedy authorized Presidential proclamation 3447, introducing the embargo on Cuba that exists today. (Dunning 214 – 215) By the mid 1970s, the fundamental goal of destroying or dismantling the Cuban Revolution seemed to be softened. However, after the election of Ronald Reagan, a new conservative program that affected all areas of domestic and foreign policy was adopted, thus hardening the U.S. policy on Cuba. (Vanderbush, 2) "Through the Reagan years, the Cuban American National Foundation (CANF) was becoming increasingly powerful and more autonomous in making policy related to Cuba." (Vanderbush, 3) In the 1990s, Castro opened his nation for foreign investments. In response, the United States passed the Cuban Democracy Act (CDA), "add[ing] provisions by strengthening and extending the reach of the embargo," and preventing any trade with Cuba. (Dunning, 217- 218)

On March 12, 1996, in response to Cuba's downing of two American civilian aircraft, President Clinton signed the Helms-Burton Act into law. From the time of its introduction, the Helms-Burton Act enjoyed almost complete support from Republicans and gained widespread support among Democrats. The Act has caused the United States to become the target of significant international criticism, however. (Dunning 213-223) According to the United States, since its implementation, several foreign companies have violated the Act. (Dunning, 228)

Violated or not, the fact is that economic and other American interests are at stake. The current U.S-Cuban relationship has affected other aspects of U.S relations with third-world countries. However slowly, there are already changes underway in Cuba. More and more countries are demanding to see Cuba integrated into the international community. Some 71% of Americans – with an even higher concentration of supporters in Miami – feel that the time has come for the United States to review and renew its relationship with its southern neighbor. Overall, maintaining the embargo on Cuba is a rather self-debasing act, which compromises (or even undermines) the American international image.

The Future of U.S.-Cuba Relations and the Lessons to be Learned

The U.S. Government has recently begun to display several signs of a cautious willingness to cooperate and compromise with Cuba. When building the international coalition to launch the war against global terrorism, the United States attempted to bring partners, including Cuba into the fray.

Cuba has always maintained a willingness to negotiate with the United States – but this willingness is dependent upon equal treatment, mutual respect, and adequate benefits. Lately, globalization, world trade, and political and economic cooperation between industrialized countries have grown dramatically. At the same time, it is clear that third-world nations, with all their difficulties, are somewhat marginalized from these global benefits.

Cuban society is undergoing a period of readjustment that could still cause some tension. Keeping the spirit of the Revolution alive is an important part of the Cuban people and their culture. Therefore, rebuilding a relationship with the United States (a country that does not share such values) will be a long and arduous process. From the Cuban perspective, there is still a lot of skepticism over whether Americans would actually fulfill their promises – even if a relationship of mutual respect could ever be reached.

As childish as it may seem, the U.S-Cuban contest comes down to a battle of wills, where one government is intent upon making the other do its bidding. In early 2000, President Bill Clinton suggested that every time he was prepared to improve relations, Castro did something that made it impossible for him to proceed. The Cuban leader, Clinton concluded, did not really want improved relations. (Robinson, 117-118)

For the United States, it was easier to normalize relations with Vietnam and China (despite the cost of 54,000 American soldiers' lives) than it has been to smooth out relations with Cuba. Clinton has moved to allow direct flights, increased access for news organization, and person-to-person contact and made changes in remittances. However, the President cannot dodge Congress on the ultimate question of the embargo – which has been codified (an important and often overlooked point). Essentially, Cuban policy is now largely an issue of domestic politics. Now and in the future, struggles between the President and Congress (along with the assertiveness of Cuban-Americans and other policy entrepreneurs) in the legislature are likely to be every bit as critical as developments on the island of Cuba itself. (Vanderbush, 11)

While there have been hints of a rapprochement with Cuba, the road towards normalization seems a long one. Events such as the explosive situation in the Middle East, the Argentinean crash, and the questionable state of the post-Chavez Venezuelan democracy, however, suggest that action on the part of the U.S. should come sooner rather than later.

Cuba has been a bastion of Latin American resistance to U.S. influence and if the U.S. does not take serious steps to normalize relations with this country soon, others may follow its lead.

The Transition to Democracy in Nicaragua
By **Ksenija Arsic**
November, 2002

Introduction

Two challenges have dominated Latin American politics in the twentieth century. The first is the struggle to overcome persistent poverty and economic underdevelopment and the second is the effort to create and consolidate democratic forms of government. In many cases, implementing open and so-called free elections, freedom of press, and party organizing completed this transitional period. Yet, visible poverty, inequality, and corruption remain the core of the problems for the majority of Latin American countries undergoing the process of democratization. In Latin America today, concerns about the process center around not only the threat of authoritarian regression, but on the quality of large-scale economic and social reform, stronger and more complex civil societies, and processes of globalization, as well.[209]

The Spanish conquests of the region – coupled with its methods of rule and tradition – have largely influenced the development of Latin American society. Economically, Spanish mercantilism has made Latin America dependent upon outside resources and has given rise to corruption and evaporation of trust in the government. In the centuries that followed, Latin America was systematically drained of its

---

[209] Hillman, Richard S. "Understanding Contemporary Latin America," Chapter 14: "Trends and Prospects," by Hillman, Richard, Pg. 375-383. Boulder, London, Lynne Rienner Publishers, 2001.

resources, its indigenous peoples exploited, and its economy under invested. Latin American independence came amidst widespread chaos with the fall of the throne in Spain. The region suffered through constant pressure from the Caudillos to fill the vacuum of power. Liberation also allowed for increasing investment by France, England, and the U.S. – allowing the three countries to control the developing Latin American economy.[210]

Despite the liberal social revolution that was initiated, the power of the church, the military, and the "Criollo" Oligarchy remained intact.[211] A tendency toward authoritarianism and the competition for power was intense. The absence of a unified central power what was the Spanish crown left Latin American countries unprepared to build their nations.[212]

Latin America was (and to a great degree, still is) governed by the law that applies to few of the ruling elite and former military leaders. An unequal distribution of wealth, a high crime rate, widespread violence, and lack of equal treatment under the law undermines faith in the government and gives little recourse to ordinary people.[213] In order to have sustainable democracy, it is necessary to have the support of the people. Faith in the economy and social equality produces faith in the government – and this is exactly what Latin American countries are attempting to achieve. As Hillman wrote, "the opportunities for this region continue to be great and, with vast natural and human resources, with cultural diversity that produces unity, with recognition of the need for democratization and with expansion of the economy, Latin America will be able to overcome its present struggle during the process of democratization."[214]

Despite promising cases such as Mexico and Chile, there has been a general impression that consolidation of democracy in Latin America is still in the early stages. The Free Trade Agreement and official support for democracy from the United States of America still begs the question: "Can Latin America evolve to the level of stability required

---

[210] Ibid. Chapter 2: "Latin America: A geographic Preface," by Price Marie, and Chapter 3: "The Historical Context," by Rene de la Pedraja Pg. 11-58.
[211] Hillman, Richard S. "Understanding Contemporary Latin America," 2nd ed. Chapter 3: "The Historical Context," by Rene de la Pedraja Pg. 58. Boulder, London, Lynne Rienner Publishers, 2001.
[212] Ibid. Chapter 4: "Latin American Politics," by D'Agostino, Thomas J. Pg. 64.
[213] Ibid. Chapter 14: "Trends and Prospects," by Hillman, Richard, Pg. 380-381.
[214] Ibid. Pg. 382.

for equal partnership in an integrated hemisphere?"[215] How fragile is the democratization of Latin America, in particular, in Nicaragua? What are the perspectives of democracy in Nicaragua? In order to try to answer these questions, this paper will first examine some of the definitions of democracy. Second, a brief overview of the history and the process of democratization in Nicaragua will be presented. Finally, this paper will analyze some of the facts regarding the problems as well as the future of democracy in Latin America and, in particular, Nicaragua.

---

[215] Hillman, Richard S. "Understanding Contemporary Latin America," 2nd ed. Chapter 3: "The Historical Context," by Rene de la Pedraja Pg. 379. Boulder, London, Lynne Rienner Publishers, 2001.

Definitions of Democracy, Transition, and Consolidation

For centuries, any attempt to set up the ultimate democracy (a term derived from the Greek word's "demos" - people and "kratia" - power) has been met with struggle.[216] From the ancient civilizations of Greece and Rome all the way to the government of the United States, the primary goal has been to achieve complete and true democracy. Vast numbers of theories and definitions concerning democracy have been offered and most scholars agree that there are a few essential characteristics that must be present in a political system for it even to be considered democratic.[217]

The crucial characteristic of a legitimate democracy, according to Dahl, is that it allows people to freely make choices without government intervention.[218] Another necessary characteristic is political equality and majority rule. With political equality must also come economic equality. For this equality to occur, all people must be subject to the same laws, be granted equal civil rights, and be allowed to freely express their ideas. In addition, minority rights must be respected and free elections (meaning that every vote must count equally) must be held at regular intervals.[219] As Dahl points out, there is a variety of democracies – and they fall under four specific categories: Primary, Referendum, Committee and Representative. The best possible form of

---

[216] ARTEL Webster Search, www.humanities,uchicago,edu/forms_unrest/Webster.form.html, visited on June 26, 2002.
[217] Dahl, Robert A. "After The Revolution, Authority In a Good Society," Pg. 59-104. New Haven and London: Yale University Press. 1970.
[218] Ibid. Pg. 8.
[219] Ibid. Pg. 8- 58.

democracy, Dahl believes, is a polyarchy – or the closest model of Representative Democracy to an ideal.[220]

> *The real world issue has not turned out to be whether a majority, much less 'the' majority, will act in a tyrannical way through democratic procedures to impose its will on a (or the) minority. Instead, the more relevant question is the extent to which various minorities in a society will frustrate the ambitions of one another with the passive acquiescence or indifference of a majority of adults or voters...if there is anything to be said for the processes that actually distinguish democracy (or polyarchy) from dictatorship...the distinction comes...to being one between government by a minority and government by minorities. As compared with the political processes of a dictatorship, the characteristics of polyarchy greatly extend the number, size, and diversity of the minorities whose preferences will influence the outcome of governmental decisions.* [221]

Although complete and true democracy is almost impossible to achieve, if the elite rule, it cannot even exist through elections.[222]. In order for democracy to be sustained, the government must be kept in check – if not via constitutional powers, then by the people themselves. This need calls for the general populace to be educated and literate; a people that constantly questions its government. Without education, the population lacks the political ambitions or ideas to make the government better.[223]

According to Adam Przeworski, "Democracy is a system in which parties lose elections. There are parties: divisions of interest, values and opinions. There is competition, organized by rules. And there are periodic winners and losers."[224] Moreover, as Przerowski further points

---

[220] Ibid. Pg. 78.
[221] Dahl, Robert A. "A Preface To Democratic Theory," Pg. 133. , Chicago and London: The University of Chicago Press. The University of Toronto Press, Toronto 5. Canada. 1956.
[222] Dahl, Robert A. "After The Revolution, Authority In a Good Society," Pg. 4-5. New Haven and London: Yale University Press. 1970.
[223] Dahl, Robert A. "A Preface To Democratic Theory," Pg. 81. , Chicago and London: The University of Chicago Press. The University of Toronto Press, Toronto 5. Canada. 1956.
[224] Przeworski, Adam " "Democracy and the Market: Political and Economic Reforms in Eastern Europe and Latin America," Pg. 10. New York: Cambridge University

out, the quality of a democracy depends on citizen participation in governmental concerns.

In respect to a transition to democracy, Przerowski suggests that, "democracy means that all groups must subject their interests to uncertainty. It is this very act of alienation of control over outcomes of conflicts that constitutes the decisive step toward democracy." [225] Transition to democracy, according to O'Donnell and Schmitter, is the period between one political regime and another – wherein a country moves from an authoritarian ruling body to a democratic one. The process of democratization should not be confused with the process of liberalization. Liberalization simply refers to the overthrowing of a tyrannical government. The process, itself, may lead to the rule of another tyrannical government. Democratization is itself a form of liberalization as it leads specifically to the implementation of a democracy. It is also important to note the concept of "pact".[226] According to O'Donnell and Scmiter:

> "A pact can be defined as an explicit, but not always publicly explicated or justified, agreement among a select set of actors which seeks to define (or better to redefine) rules governing the exercise of power on the basis of mutual guarantees for the 'vital interests' of those entering into it. Such pacts may be of prescribed duration or merely contingent upon ongoing consent. In any case, they are often initially regarded as a temporary solutions intended to avoid certain worrisome outcomes, and, perhaps, to pave the way for more permanent arrangements for the resolution of conflicts."[227]

By O'Donnelli and Scmitter's analysis, it can be noted that each moment of the process of democratization has its own set of rules and its own subset of actors trying to establish various pacts during

---

Press, 1991.
[225] O' Donnell, Guillermo, Schmitter, Philipe C. and Witehead Laurence, "Transitions from Authoritarian Rule, Comparative Perspectives," Chapter 2, by Porzeworski, Adam, "Some Problems in the Study of the Transition to Democracy," Pg. 60. The Woodrow Wilson International Center for Scholars, The Johns Hopkins University Press, 1986.
[226] O'Donnell, Guillermo, Schmiter, Philipe C. "Transition from Authoritarian Rule: Tentative Conclusions About Uncertain Democracies," Ibid. Pg. 7-8. and Pg. 37-39 Baltimore and London: The John Hopkins University Press, 1986.
[227] Ibid. Pg. 37.

negotiations. The essence of democracy is that no one's interests can be guaranteed and that democracy is about compromise and consensus.

The establishment and consolidation of democratic regimes has been a difficult and elusive challenge in Latin America. While discussing the consolidation of democracy, Juan J. Linz and Alfred C.Stepan write that, although free elections are a necessary condition of democracy, this itself is not sufficient to achieving the ideal.[228] In order to achieve a consolidated democracy, some degree of autonomy and independence of civil and political society must exist. Therefore, the first arena of a civil society must display legal, basic freedoms of person, free and nonviolent competition among its leaders (with a periodical check of their rule), and participation of its citizens and state of law in order to be considered consolidated. The second arena, as Linz and Stepan suggest, refers to the economic society that mediates between state and market.[229]

Having made the transition to democracy, Latin American countries are now faced with the problem of consolidating democracy for what Przeworski writes:

Democracy is consolidated when under given political and economic conditions a particular system of institutions becomes the only game in town, when no one can imagine acting outside the democratic institutions, when all losers want to do is to try again within the same institutions under which they have just lost. [230]

Latin American democratic transition and consolidation in post-authoritarian and post-civil-war conditions represents the unfinished journey. Many believe that, in the first months after a transition, the survival of the successor regime depends on swift and firm action against pro-authoritarian officials and their followers – carried out via prosecution – in order to establish or restore a basic trust in the new government. In a sense, a new democracy needs to show its capability in the handling of past abuses.[231] Transition to democracy, as

---

[228] Linz, Juan J. and Alfred Stepan, "Problems of Democratic Transition and Consolidation, Southern Europe, South America, and Post-Communist Europe," Pg. 4. Baltimore and London: The Johns Hopkins University Press, 1996.

[229] Ibid. Pg. 7-15.

[230] Przeworski, Adam, "Democracy and the Market: Political and Economic Reforms in Eastern Europe and Latin America," Pg. 26. New York: Cambridge University Press, 1991.

[231] O'Donnell, Guillermo, Schmiter, Philipe C. "Transition from Authoritarian Rule:

O'Donnelli and Schmiter point out, has too much uncertainty about its capabilities and intentions. Nevertheless, when the transition has passed and people have learned mutual tolerance and compromise, then it is possible for the process of democratization to succeed.[232]

Tentative Conclusions About Uncertain Democracies," Pg. 39-56. Baltimore and London: The Johns Hopkins University Press, 1986.

[232] Ibid. Pg. 72.

Nicaragua

Nicaragua is a country that borders the Caribbean Sea and the North Pacific Ocean. It has long struggled to establish its own existence and significance to the world as a whole. After the Nicaraguan Revolution overthrew long-time-dictator Anastasio Somoza in the late 1970's – and following an economic collapse and civil war that was waged throughout the 1980's – Nicaragua began the 1990's under the leadership of Violeta Chamorro. The process of reconciliation, rebuilding a devastated infrastructure, and reviving an almost non-existent private sector had begun.[233] In order to better understand this country's long history, it is crucial to outline the relationship between Nicaragua and the U.S. Another major influence to consider is that of the Roman Catholic Church.

The concept of democracy and the promotion of that democracy to the rest of the world is a central tenant of U.S. foreign policy. Many observers believe that American policymakers have viewed democracy as an export commodity and, in the case that democracy needs to be defended, armed intervention in the affairs of another state is justified. In reality, the use of force is the antithesis of proper democratic decision-making, especially when it is applied as an excuse to invade another country.

Democracy cannot simply be shipped from one country to another and start to "grow". Every state has its own specific characteristics and they need to be taken into consideration if the process is ever to come

---

[233] Hillman, Richard S. "Understanding Contemporary Latin America," 2nd ed. Chapter 3: "The Historical Context," by Rene de la Pedraja MAP 3.3 Pg. 52- 53. Boulder, London, Lynne Rienner Publishers, 2001. See also: http://www.internationalreports.net/theamericas/nicaragua/2002/Presidentbolanos.html, International Reports Net, the Washington Times: "Nicaragua 2002" June 26, 2002.

to fruition. Democracy can, in fact, be achieved by every nation – but not if it is imposed upon them by a misunderstanding outside force.[234]

Throughout the years, the U.S. has played a significant role in the internal affairs of Nicaragua while trying to promote democracy. At first, the U.S. government had appeared much more concerned about the presence of Soviet and Cuban influence on Nicaragua than with the idea of building democracy. The American government made little attempt to consider the needs or interests of the Nicaraguan people and, as a result, the effort to impose a democracy never succeeded.[235]

Roman Catholicism came to Nicaragua in the sixteenth century with the Spanish conquest and remained the established faith until 1939. The Roman Catholic Church had a privileged legal status and Church authorities usually supported the political status quo – until 1900, when the Church became disorganized.

> *During this period in the 19th century there occurred bitter infighting for political control in which the clericals wanted the Church to continue to have direct influence in state affairs and the anticlerical wanted to push the Church out of state affairs and control it in some ways.* [236]

In most countries, the Church had lost its land, its wealth, its control over education, birth registry, marriage etc. and come out of the struggle clearly less influential and poorer; constantly having to defend its remaining power.[237] Over the course of the past 30 years, there has been a "politicization of religion" wherein the political involvement of

---

[234] Lowenthal, Abraham F. "Exporting Democracy: The United States and Latin America, Case Studies,"Chapter 5, by Tulchin, Joseph S. and Knut Walter, "Nicaragua: The Limits of Intervention," Pg. 111- 112. and Chapter 10: "The United States and Latin American Democracy: Learning from History," by Lowenthal Abraham F. Pg. 280. Baltimore and London: The Johns Hopkins University Press, 1991.

[235] Ibid Chapter 5, by Tulchin, Joseph S. and Knut Walter, "Nicaragua: The Limits of Intervention," Pg.112.

[236] Archbishop Marcos McGrath, C.S.C, "Latin America: Dependency or Interdependence?" "The Role of the Catholic Church in Latin American Development," by Michael Novak and Michael P. Jackson, Pg.125. Washington, D.C: American Enterprise Institute for Public Policy Research, 1985.

[237] Tannenbaum, Frank. "Government and Politics in Latin America, A Reader," Part 1: by Peter G. Snow "Religion in Latin America," Pg. 116, Holt: Rinehart and Winston, Inc. 1967.

the Church has become divided.[238] As an economically diminished institution, the Church was forced to support social hierarchies and uneven distributions of power and wealth in order to survive. Such conditions threatened to seriously distance the majority poor of Latin America. Therefore, the Church began to distance itself from the elites. This sudden shift brought challenges for the Catholic Church as well as the wider international context. These challenges lead to vast revisions in theology brought about by Vatican II, emphasizing the universal rights for a decent standard of living, education, and political participation.[239]

The 1970s and 1980s were years of religious ferment in Nicaragua that are often connected with political conflict. Encouraged by the spirit of liberal renovation that was sweeping trough Latin American Catholicism, a new generation of Nicaraguan Roman Catholic Church officials and lay-activists attempted to make the Roman Catholic Church more democratic and more sensitive to the plight of the poor majority. Influenced by the radical doctrines of Liberation Theology, Roman Catholic clergy and lay-activists were drawn into the movement opposed to the injustices of the Somoza regime. Many developed links with the Sandinista National Liberation Front (FSLN). No previous Latin American revolution had had such broad religious support as that of the Sandinistas. Even the Roman Catholic Bishops openly backed the anti-Somosa movement in its final phase.[240]

Common sense is that the clergy should not practice violence and the Church should work for nonviolent change. Violent revolutions rarely bring about the positive change they seek. It is also true that, while violence may be necessary for people in order to rid themselves of an abusive government, it is highly unorthodox for churches to encourage it. Once the Sandinistas took power, the polarization of the Revolution split the Church. The Christian tendency was introduced and the historical view of the Catholic Church as the sole moral authority in society was challenged.[241]

---

[238] Human Affairs, No.7, 2/1997, Pg. 184. "The Traditional and Present Role of the Church in Latin America," article by Pawlikova Lucia.

[239] Ibid. Pg. 185.

[240] Journal of Latin American Studies, No.17, Year 1985-86. Pg. 341 and 349. "The Catholic Hierarchy in the Nicaraguan Revolution," by Williams, Philip J.

[241] Thomas W. Walker: "Nicaragua Without Illusions: Regime Transition and Structural Adjustment in the 1990s" Chapter 14: "The Church," Pg. 236-237, by Andrew J. Stein, Wilmington, DE: A Scholarly Resources Inc. Imprint, 1997.

Nicaragua's main guerilla group was the Frente Sandinista de Liberación Nacional (FSLN).[242] They initially formed in 1961 but then split up in the late 1970's because of tactical disagreements. In 1979, however, the ruling Somoza regime had become so unpopular that the FSLN reunited to take power – amidst widespread support. A provisional FSLN government ruled until 1984 and was then democratically elected for a five-year term. In the 1990 election, the FSLN lost power but still sustains a large base of support. Throughout most of the time the FSLN was formally in power of the state, Nicaragua was under extreme pressure from the U.S. – the latter country imposing harsh economic sanctions and supporting a counterrevolutionary coup known as Contras.

The official ideology of the FLSN was that of Marxism. The decline of this ideology was visible in the reality and practice of the Sandinistas by the middle of the decade, however.[243] At the time the Sandinistas lost the 1990 election, a wave of violence had erupted in Nicaragua. Armed fighters were roughly organized into what was called the Resistencia Nicaragüense (RN).[244] Unrest was caused by the fact that people were tired of waiting for a solution – a solution that was delayed largely by the chronically unequal distribution of wealth and power that was categorically in the hands of the economic elite and corrupt governmental regimes. Furthermore, there was strong evidence of the repression and censorship of military dictatorships along with the violent silencing of any political opposition. Rebel armies began to spring up. These movements hoped for the eventual transition to political democracy.

As Armony points out, another important element that fueled the Contra counter-revolution was the exclusion of indigenous people. In the eyes of the U.S., FSLN's major shortcoming was its failure to address the problem of indigenous people. According to Joankin analysis, the Sandinista Front of National Liberation government failed to keep its promise to secure formal tenure for individual small producers and cooperative members who represented critical components of the revolutionary alliance[245]:

---

[242] Ibid. Chapter 9: "The FSLN" Pg. 149-199, by Gary Prevost.

[243] Thomas W.Walker: "Nicaragua Without Illusions: Regime Transition and Structural Adjustment in the 1990s" Chapter 14: "The Church," Pg. 149-199. by Andrew J.Stein, Wilmington, DE: A Scholarly Resources Inc. Imprint, 1997.

[244] Ibid. Chapter 12: "The Former Contras" Pg. 204-205, edited by Armony Ariel C.

[245] Chapter 6: "Agrarian Policy" Pg. 97. by Jon Jonakin:

During the 1980s the Sandanista Agrarian Reform (SAR) had substantially altered Somoza –era structure of land tenure as thousands of peasants and rural wage workers acquired rights to former latifundio estates. Land redistribution, along with policies that expanded access to education, agricultural technology, producer credit, and political participation, created what some argued were the 'structural preconditions' for a democracy that aspired to more than an open electoral process."[246]

As a result, Nicaragua was faced with a wave of uprisings against the government by former members of the armed opposition (or Contras) and by groups of former Sandinista army officers alleging the government's failure to deliver on promises of land, credit, housing, and other promised benefits.[247]

Nicaragua is an extremely poor country with an estimated per capita gross domestic product of $454.[248] The economy is predominantly agricultural, dependent upon sugar, beef, coffee, and seafood exports, with some light manufacturing. Hurricane Mitch reduced the annual growth rate for 1998 from 6% before the hurricane to 4% after. Despite this setback, the economy grew 6.3% in 1999 and the inflation rate dropped from 18.5% to 11.5. The unemployment rate is officially reported as 11% – though, according to a report of some nongovernmental organizations, the rate of unemployment and underemployment combined is estimated at 40-50%.[249]

Today, private foreign investment in Nicaragua has started to increase. Unresolved property disputes and unclear land deals that were practiced during the massive confiscation effort conducted by the Sandinista government of the 1980's has prevented quicker economic growth, however. The many rebel organizations have become peaceful political parties in a relatively democratic Nicaraguan society.

---

[246] Ibid.
[247] Thomas W.Walker: "Nicaragua Without Illusions: Regime Transition and Structural Adjustment in the1990s" Chapter 6: "Agrarian Policy," Pg. 97-126, by Jon Jonakin, Wilmington, DE: A Scholarly Resources Inc. Imprint, 1997.
[248] See: http://worldpolicy.org/americas/nicaragua/2001Nicaragua-election-background.html, "Nicaragua Elections," visited on August 15, 2002.
[249] Ibid.

The transition to democracy was peaceful but the defeat of the Sandinista regime did not end the debate about democracy in Nicaragua.[250]

As mentioned earlier, the United States has been a powerful external factor in Nicaragua's democratization. The transition process of Nicaragua, writes Armony, did not exhibit balance between sides but was clearly dominated by elites and United States interests.[251] The Chamorro administration and the elites of the country strongly promoted the disarmament of the Contras but did not balance this with any serious response to the needs of the people who were fighting and were therefore unable to sustain peace. The government implemented economic liberalization but failed to implement any support for the former fighters – a failure that only added to impoverishment and furthered postwar violence.[252] A relatively strong civil society emerged after the Sandinista period had ended. The Contras had access to a wide range of non-violent alternatives during the process of negotiations but, when the government did not respond positively, the peaceful approach to civil society became insufficient and violence was an increasingly attractive option.[253] The need for violence resulted in a significant setback for the Contras and their political pull during the democratization process. Groups that use violence in a democratic system are unlikely to gather mass support, no matter how substantially their demands are democratic.

A lack of will to seriously negotiate on the part of the Chamorro administration and the Contras brought yet more obstruction to the hope of peace and justice.[254]

> *It would appear, at least in the case of Nicaragua, that foreign intervention had been damaging to civic culture. It can be argued that U.S. interventions (initially against Zelaya, Zeledon, and Sandino, then on behalf of the Somosas, and*

---

[250] Lowenthal, Abraham F. "Exporting Democracy: The United States and Latin America, Case Studies," Chapter 5, by Tulchin, Joseph S. and Knut Walter, "Nicaragua: The Limits of Intervention," Pg. 131-138. Baltimore and London: The Johns Hopkins University Press, 1991.

[251] Thomas W.Walker: "Nicaragua Without Illusions: Regime Transition and Structural Adjustment in the1990s" Chapter 12: "The Former Contras," Pg. 203-204, by Armony, Ariel C., Wilmington, DE: A Scholarly Resources Inc. Imprint, 1997.

[252] Ibid. Pg. 205.

[253] Ibid. Pg. 212.

[254] Ibid. Pg.209.

finally against the Sandinistas), however successful they may have been in achieving Washington's short-term objectives, damaged Nicaraguan politics in at least two ways. First, they created a tendency on the part of some politicians to look to the gringos for solutions to their problems rather than to engage in negotiation and compromise, the essence of any democratic system. The Conservatives did this early in the century, the monied elite and opposition Microparties continued this tradition in the 1980s, and the anti-Sandinista right took up the baton from 1990 onward. This tendency, in turn, led to frequent polarization, impasse, and violence. Second, by providing yet another dimension for disagreement and conflict, nationalist-collaborationist squabbling arising out of frequent interventions may well have been one of the major factors contributing to the extreme fragmentation of Nicaragua's party system as seen in the mid-1990s.[255]

Strong and active civil society is the key for democracy. While America dominates the international political arena, promoting its democracy to the rest of the world, it perpetuates a number of its own problems. With such inconsistencies in mind, one is inevitably lead to the question of, how, then, will countries in Latin America achieve high civic engagement while well-established democracies are already experiencing similar problems?

The U.S. has been a major player and anxious prospector in Nicaraguan politics for many years. What the U.S. government unfortunately fails to realize, however, is that the process of democratization is a gradual one. There is no prescription or user's manual for democracy. In order for the process of democratization to be successful, respect for the sovereignty of the country, its traditions, and the culture of its people must be taken into consideration. Every country is unique. Each deserves the opportunity to build democracy on its own and in its best-suited way.[256]

---

[255] Thomas W.Walker: "Nicaragua Without Illusions: Regime Transition and Structural Adjustment in the 1990's", Reflections," by Thomas W. Walker, Pg. 298.Wilmington, DE: A Scholarly Resources Inc. Imprint, 1997.

[256] See: http://web.inter.nl.net/users/Paul.Treanor/,document Index, "Why Democracy is wrong" visited on December 21, 2002.

Conclusion

"Violeta Chamorro's ascension to power was accompanied by hopes and promises of economic improvement... It was also true, however, that under the transitional regime headed by Violeta Chamorro social goods were distributed differently than they were under the FSLN. Benefactors of either distributional scheme were apt to reward the government success, even if they stopped short of identifying political with the party in power – even, in fact, if they identified with an opposing political faction. Governments in Nicaragua were able to generate support for the larger system by distributing benefits to the population and by successfully managing the national economy. Many informal workers, however, bore the brunt of the protracted economic crisis that began in the late 1980s and continued into the 1990s. Their suffering helped to explain why system support was so low among this part of the population."[257]

Today's world, with all its trembling uncertainty and sudden change, can be, at times, overwhelming. Globalization, world trade, and political and economic cooperation betwen industrialized countries have grown dramatically. Even as this trend progresses, it has become clear that third-world nations have remained somehow marginalized when it comes to these global benefits. Although the Free Trade Area of the Americas represents the kind of integrative trend so desperately needed in the West, Latin American countries still have a

---

[257] Thomas W. Walker: "Nicaragua Without Illusions: Regime Transition and Structural Adjustment in the 1990's", Chapter 16: "The Urban Informal Economic Sector", by John G. Speer. Pg. 276. Wilmington, DE: A Scholarly Resources Inc. Imprint, 1997.

long way to go when it comes to achieving stable democracy and international significance.

The opportunities for this region continue to be staggering. With vast natural and human resources, with the diversity of culture that produces unity, with the recognition of the need for democratization, and with the expansion of its economy, Latin America should eventually be able to overcome its present struggle during the process of democratization.[258]

> *In November 2001, Enrique Bolaños was elected President of Nicaragua: the third democratic transition of power in the post-Sandinista era. In the historic elections, the Constitutional Liberal Party) of Mr. Bolaños given an overwhelming mandate by the people of Nicaragua to maintain a free, democratic and market-driven society.* [259]

The focus of President Bolaños is to continue the nation's substantial growth and economic development that began in 1990 with Nicaragua's successful transition to democracy create more jobs and to make Nicaragua an even more attractive country in which to invest. Furthermore, President Bolaños is clearly determined to completely eliminate corruption at all levels of society – from the highest levels of government to the streets to the private sector. It seems that the traditional corruption of Nicaragua's governmental officials is coming to an end. For the first time in Nicaragua's history, these officials have been found guilty of criminal charges and will face jail time and official disgrace. This could improve a level of confidence and trust in President Bolaños' administration and, more importantly, could restore Nicaraguans' hope for a better future.[260]

---

[258] Hillman, Richard S. "Understanding Contemporary Latin America," Chapter 14: "Trends and Prospects," by Hillman, Richard, Pg. 382. Boulder, London, Lynne Rienner Publishers, 2001.

[259] See:http://www.internationalreports.net/theamericas/nicaragua/2002/Presidentbolanos.html, International Reports Net, The Washington Times: "Nicaragua 2002" visited on June 26, 2002.

[260] Ibid.

Bibliography

ARTEL Webster Search. June 26, 2002. Webster Dictionary www.humanities,uchicago,edu/forms_unrest/Webster.form.html

Archbishop McGrath, Marcos C.S.C. "Latin America: Dependency or Interdependence?" Washington, D.C. American Enterprise Institute for Public Policy Research. 1985.

Dahl, Robert A. "After The Revolution: Authority In a Good Society." New Haven and London. Yale University Press. 1970.

"A Preface To Democratic Theory." Chicago and London. The University of Chicago Press. The University of Toronto Press. Toronto. 1956.

Hillman, Richard S. "Understanding Contemporary Latin America." Boulder, London. Lynne Rienner Publishers. 2001.

International Reports Net. "Nicaragua 2002." *The Washington Times*. June 26,2002.

http://www.internationalreports.net/theamericas/nicaragua/2002/Presidentbolanos.html

Linc, Juan J. & Stepan, Alfred. "Problems of Democratic Transition and Consolidation: Southern Europe, South America, and Post-Communist Europe." Baltimore and London. The Johns Hopkins University Press. 1996.

Lowenthal, Abraham F. "Exporting Democracy: The United States and Latin America." Baltimore and London. The Johns Hopkins University Press. 1991.

Lucia, Pawlikova. "The Traditional and Present Role of the Church in Latin America." *Human Affairs*, No.7, 2/1997.

O'Donnell, Guillermo & Schmiter, Philipe C. "Transition from Authoritarian Rule: Tentative Conclusions About Uncertain Democracies." Baltimore and London. The Johns Hopkins University Press. 1986.

"Transitions from Authoritarian Rule: Comparative Perspectives." The Woodrow Wilson International Center for Scholars. The Johns Hopkins University Press. 1986.

Przeworski, Adam. "Democracy and the Market: Political and Economic Reforms in Eastern Europe and Latin America." New York Cambridge University Press. 1991.

Putnam, Robert D. "Bowling Alone: The Collapse and Revival of American Community." New York. Simon and Schuster. 2000.

Tannenbaum, Frank. "Government and Politics in Latin America: A Reader." Holt, Rinehart, and Winston, Inc. 1967.

Walker, Thomas W. "Nicaragua Without Illusions: Regime Transition and Structural Adjustment in the 1990s." Wilmington, DE. A Scholarly Resources Inc. Imprint, 1997.

Williams, Philip J. "The Catholic Hierarchy in the Nicaraguan Revolution." *Journal of Latin American Studies*, No.17, Year 1985-86.

Printed in the United States
40787LVS00003B/142-174